CRU'S *Crush*

USA TODAY BESTSELLING AUTHOR

HEATHER SLADE

A complete list of Heather Slade's
series and titles is available at
the end of this book or
visit her website:
HEATHERSLADE.COM

Table of Contents

1

Cru

Beau Barrett was my best friend and, where Daphne, the woman gazing at a framed photo, was concerned, my nemesis as well. I didn't need to see it to know whose image she studied. Based on her sad expression, it was of the man I wished was here, with us, just so I could bash his fucking face in.

The two had been one of those on-again, off-again couples since they were teenagers. Every time they broke up, I hoped it would be long enough for me to have a chance with her. But, honestly, if Daphne had been the slightest bit interested in me, she wouldn't have been turning to Beau again and again and again.

"You gotta give it up, man," my oldest brother, Brix, whispered. "Beau will be back before you know it."

"Not this time, bro." I led him from the living room, down the hallway, and into a bedroom, then shut the door behind us.

Brix rested against the wall and smirked. "You keep tellin' yourself that. How long have you been crushin' on Daphne Cullen? Ten years? More?"

"Things are different now. Beau is with Samantha Marquez." Frankly, I was surprised he didn't know, given his wife, Addy, and Sam were best friends.

Brix chuckled. "Not a chance. There's no way Sam would put up with his shit." His expression changed. "Wait. Do you know where Beau is?"

Shortly after his mother's funeral, Beau had disappeared, and until I saw him in New York, I'd had no idea where he was, either. Turned out he was with Sam.

"I'm telling you; it's serious between them."

Brix pushed himself away from the wall. "So where is he?"

"C'mon. Don't ask me that. He's with Sam. That's all I can tell you right now."

"What makes you think they're serious?" Brix shook his head. "No offense at all to Sam, but I just don't see her with Beau."

I held up my phone so he could see the text I'd just received from our brother Salazar, who everyone called Snapper.

"No, shit! Beau proposed, and Sam said yes? Damn, Daphne is gonna be butthurt." Brix was practically shouting when someone pushed the door open. When he moved out of the way, I came face-to-face with the woman whose name he'd just uttered.

She spun around and raced off in the opposite direction, but not before I saw tears fill her eyes.

"What the fuck, Brix? Butthurt?" The asshole was pushing forty but sounded more like a twelve-year-old.

He grabbed my arm when I walked past him. "Let her go."

I shook my head and pulled away from his grasp. "I can't."

My brother stood in front of the door, blocking my exit, and put his hands on my shoulders. "This is going to sound corny as hell, but, Cru, you're supposed to be the leading lady, not the best friend, and for some reason, you're acting like, you know, the best friend."

I took a step back from him. "What the fuck are you talking about, Brix? The leading lady?"

"It's from a movie Addison and I watched last night. You get my point, though. You need to stop acting like the best friend, so Daphne can see you as the leading lady—err, man."

I shook my head and looked out the window. As I could've predicted, Daphne was walking on the beach, alone. Even from here, I knew she was crying.

Brix approached and stood next to me. "If you go out there now, she'll cry on your shoulder. You'll console her, and it'll be just another conversation about her and Beau. The next time you talk to her, it needs to change. No more her and Beau. Make it about her and you."

"Like it's that easy."

"Take it from me; it is if you want it bad enough." He turned to look at me. "You've loved her for as long as Beau has. And actually, I'm not sure he ever felt as strongly for her as you have."

"That doesn't mean she's ever seen me as more than a friend, or ever will," I murmured.

"Convince her otherwise."

I faced my brother and stared into his eyes. "What are you suggesting I do, Brix?"

"Leave."

"Leave? Right. You seem to forget I just rescued her from a possible kidnapping. Until they catch the people who abducted her, it's my responsibility to keep her safe."

Forty-eight hours ago, Beau had received a call from Daph, saying she was in New York City and in danger. I was with Beau at the time and volunteered to go and find her.

With the help of a private intelligence firm, we tracked her to an apartment where she was kept in a locked room. At the time of her rescue, she was the only person in the place. While I swept her out and to the nearest hospital, the owner of the firm and his team searched for clues to figure out who'd locked her in there. There wasn't a trace of evidence—no fingerprints, nothing to test DNA, even the building's CCTV footage had been destroyed.

The name Daphne gave for the man she'd traveled to New York with was an unknown alias, and so far, the description she gave hadn't yielded any clues, either. While the Manhattan police had listened to her statement, I doubted they took her seriously or intended to pursue it.

I knew Decker Ashford, the owner of the intelligence company, had a team still looking for leads. What I didn't know was who was paying them. It wouldn't sit right with me if Beau was. Nor would it with Daphne if she found out.

When I brought her to the sprawling oceanfront ranch belonging to Beau's older brother, who everyone called Press, it was because it was the safest place I could think of. The security systems there were state of the art.

Los Caballeros, my family's estate, had the same level of security. However, it would take longer for me to make arrangements for a private place for her to stay where I could also be close.

I'd been living in the guest cottage on our ranch, but it only had one bedroom.

Since Press and his wife, Luisa, were traveling and not presently here and given Daphne had stayed here many times in the past, I figured she'd feel comfortable as well as safe.

"Ready?" Brix asked.

My mouth gaped. "For what? You can't truly be suggesting I leave her here alone, not after what she's been through. Is that what you'd do with Addison?"

"You have a point."

I stared at my oldest brother and shook my head. Brix was a smart guy. Practical. Protective. After our father died, he'd taken on the role of family patriarch. So him saying I'd made a "good point" when I said

I couldn't leave her here alone was completely out of character.

"Are you okay?" I asked.

He looked out at the ocean.

"Brix?"

"Got a lot on my mind, brother."

That, I knew. He and his wife had decided to live full time on a five-thousand-acre ranch they owed in Mexico. First, they needed to finish the house they were building. The other thing in the works was Brix would soon resign from our family business, where he was the primary winemaker.

"Second thoughts?" I asked.

He turned to face me. "If you mean about you taking over at Los Caballeros, not at all." He squeezed my shoulder. "You're ready for this, Cru. You know you are."

A few months ago, when Addison's life was in turmoil, Brix had taken a leave of absence. With him gone, I was responsible for making the first label as well as the second-label varietals—which were already mine. The plan was for me to hire someone to work under me once Brix officially resigned.

So far, none of my four other brothers or one sister were interested in the job, and that meant, for the first time in the two-hundred-year history of Los Caballeros Winery, someone outside the family would be making what we'd built our reputation on. I expected Brix to balk at my siblings' lack of interest, but he didn't appear fazed.

When I glanced out the window and didn't see Daphne right away, I nearly panicked but quickly realized she was sitting on the sand.

"I should head out," I said, motioning to the bedroom door.

Brix followed me into the hallway. "I almost forgot Addison asked me to invite you to join us for dinner tonight. There are a few things we'd like to discuss." When I hesitated, he quickly added that Daphne was welcome too.

"After the butthurt comment, I doubt she'll want to."

"Yeah, it was unfortunate she heard that," he muttered.

"What was *unfortunate* was that you said it."

"Tell her I'm sorry?" he asked.

I'd suggest he tell her himself, but I doubted Daph would want to talk to him right now.

"By the way, are you still interested in my house?"

The residence he spoke of was the one he'd built on the Los Caballeros ranch. My mom still lived in the main house—the one all seven of us kids grew up in.

Brix had built his place as far from that one as he could on the five-square-mile property. Both residences were within walking distance, but neither had a view of the other.

"I am," I said when I realized he was waiting for an answer. "But you still haven't told me how much you want for it."

"I feel weird selling it to you."

I'd had just about enough of Brix's shit today and was anxious to get to Daphne, who I could see was still sitting on the sand. "Then don't."

I picked up my jacket and had my hand on the door when he grabbed my other arm. "I didn't mean it the way you're taking it. What I'm saying is Dad didn't sell me the land; it's just part of the ranch. Uncle Tryst helped me build it. I mean, how would I even figure out a price?"

"I don't know. Call an agent." I stormed out, not interested in talking about his house any longer. I had a place of my own on the property. It was small, barely nine hundred square feet, but I didn't mind. I didn't have time to take care of something bigger. Brix's house was five times the size of mine. Now that I thought about it, maybe I didn't want it, after all. The only issue was with Daphne, and I had no idea how long she'd even remain in the States. Maybe she'd want to return to Australia, where her parents lived.

"What I meant is, why don't you just move in?"

"Not interested."

"What do you mean?"

"I have my own place. I don't need you to let me stay in yours."

"We'll talk later," he said, walking in the opposite direction.

We wouldn't, but saying it was a good way to end the conversation.

The wind was fierce and the air cold today. Not unusual for January, this close to the ocean. Seeing Daphne huddled, with her arms wrapped around her knees, made me wish I'd brought a blanket out with me. Considering I was within a few feet of her, it would be stupid to turn around to get one.

"Hey," I said, sitting beside her on the sand.

"Hey, Cru," she said without looking at me.

"Brix says he's sorry for his comment."

She shrugged a shoulder. "It's what everyone thinks, right? Daphne is butthurt."

"You and Beau were together for a long time. It's understandable you'd be upset after hearing he's with someone else."

"Do you seriously think that's what upsets me?" She pushed herself off the sand, and I stood too.

My eyes scrunched. "Doesn't it?"

"God, not you too." She stormed off, but it was easy for me to stay on her heels, given I was almost a foot taller than her and my strides were twice as long.

"If it doesn't, just say so."

"Of course it doesn't," Daphne said, glancing over her shoulder.

"Hang on." When she didn't stop walking, I ran around her and blocked her way. Her head hung forward, but I put my finger on her chin and raised her face. I brushed her sandy-blonde hair from her forehead and looked into her blue-green eyes. "Why were you crying?"

Daph folded her arms and huffed. "Not for the reason you think."

I folded my arms too, more because it was fucking cold out here. "Can we go inside?"

Her head cocked. "I thought you were a surfer."

"Yeah. So?"

She shook her head and walked around me. Rather than block her again, I followed, hoping she was headed to the house.

"I never knew you were such a *sook*."

"No need to call names, and I'm hardly a wimp."

She rolled her eyes and opened the back door that led from the patio into the living room.

"Fucking Brix," I muttered.

She walked over to the counter and raised a bottle. "Fancy a cab sav?"

"Sure." I gazed out at the ocean.

"Why'd you curse Brix?" she asked, handing me a glass.

"I left before he did. He was supposed to lock up."

"He did."

Daphne sat on the sofa, grabbed the throw draped on the back, and crawled under it.

"You walked right in."

She held up her hand. "I'm programmed. You're not?"

I'd forgotten the doors would open by palm print. "I'm not here that often."

"We can share." She offered half the blanket when I sat down, rubbing my cold hands together. "Get closer," she added when I was still a foot away.

"I'm good. It's warm in here."

Before I realized what she was doing, Daphne grabbed my hand. "You're like ice." She closed the distance between us, tucked the blanket around me, then held both my hands in hers.

My arms itched to pull away. My legs too. And my cock? Hard as steel.

Daphne had no idea the torture she was putting me through or how much easier on me it would've been if she'd just let me continue freezing my ass off.

2

Daphne

The tension reverberating off Cru's body was almost palpable. If he'd pressed to know why I was crying earlier, I would have had to admit his reluctance to touch me was one reason. Cru and I had always been close. God, we'd known each other since we were teenagers. He'd never hesitated to hug me, rub my shoulders, nudge me with his elbow, or even curl up under a blanket with me when we watched a movie. Why had that changed all of a sudden?

Was it because I wasn't with Beau anymore and Cru didn't want to give me the wrong idea? Did he think I was so desperate for companionship that I'd expect him to pick up where my other boyfriend had left off? Did Cru, who I believed knew me better than just about anyone else, think I was the kind of girl who was afraid of being single? That I always had to have a boyfriend?

Another reason for my tears was Brix's comment. I hated that everyone—not just Cru—thought I was devastated by Beau's relationship with Sam. It wasn't that I didn't care. In fact, I was happy for them.

Finally, the thing weighing heaviest on my mind was what I would do with the rest of my life. That worry wasn't new. Two weeks ago, I'd turned twenty-six—the same age my mum was when I was born.

I'd gone to university, graduated, and went on to get my master's in Viticulture and Enology from UC Davis, but had done nothing with it. No doubt, my parents hoped I'd return to Australia and work for them, but they were well aware I didn't want to. I loved them, but they didn't own a *winery*. Instead, it was one of the largest privately held global wine-making and distribution businesses in the world. An MBA would've served me far better if that had been the kind of work I wanted to do.

The problem was no one wanted to hire me. Or that's what I believed. I hadn't looked for a job, either here, on the Central Coast, or in Napa or Sonoma, because I knew the kind of work I wanted didn't exist.

The only way I could make wine for a small vintner was if I purchased vineyard property myself. Even then, I'd have to hire someone to help me for the first five years at least.

I sighed, rested my head against the sofa, and closed my eyes.

"What?" Cru asked.

I opened one and glanced at him. "What, what?"

"The sigh."

"I'm hungry." It wasn't a lie, but it was misleading. I was starving for a life, not food.

"So, uh…"

"What?" I said like he had, sitting up.

"Brix and Addy invited us over for dinner tonight."

"And?"

"Do you want to go?"

I shrugged. "Sure. If you do." Maybe Brix would know of a vineyard owner in search of an apprentice winemaker.

"Can you wait that long?"

I studied him. "To ask about a job?"

Cru's forehead furrowed. "I was talking about eating since you said you're hungry. I didn't know you were looking for a job. Do you think…?"

"What?" I repeated.

"Are you planning on staying here?"

"If by here you mean at Seahorse, then no. If you mean on the Central Coast, it depends on whether I can find something to do with myself."

"I thought after…"

"Bloody hell, Cru, finish your sentences."

"What you went through. I wondered if you'd want to return to Australia."

I raised a brow. "You do remember the guy I was with was an Aussie, right?" It was stupid of me to think I'd be safe with a stranger, regardless of where he was from. When I thought about what could have happened to me, I shuddered.

"Daph?"

"Sorry. What were you saying?"

"Nothing. It was you who said you wanted to talk to Brix about a job."

"Seems time I got one, doesn't it?" I rested against the sofa again and shut my eyes.

"What kind of work do you want to do?"

I opened one like I had before and sighed again. "The kind I doubt exists. At least how I want to do it."

Cru turned his body toward me. "Wine-making?"

"I know I sound like a spoiled ankle biter, but I want to make my own."

"Interesting."

"You're probably going to suggest I purchase a vineyard, but I've looked, and there are none I'd want to take on."

"That's not what I had in mind."

"Do you know someone who's looking?" I asked.

Cru nodded. "Los Cab."

"Very funny. Are you telling me you're leaving?"

"Not me. Brix."

My eyes opened wide. "Why?"

"He and Addy want to live in Mexico. They're building a house on the property Uncle Tryst gave them as a wedding gift."

"I don't see Brix giving up wine-making."

"I didn't, either, but he's set on it."

I looked at the time. It was late for lunch, but too long until dinner. While I hadn't felt hungry for food a few minutes ago, I did now. "Stave is open, right?"

"What day is it?"

I smiled. Cru's quirk was never remembering the day of the week. "Friday."

"Then, yeah."

"I could go for some tapas." Stave was a wine bar and tasting room in the village of Cambria, which was about a ten-minute drive north from where we were. Cru's sister, Alex, and her best friend, Peyton, owned it.

He stood. "Ready when you are."

"I, um…"

"Are you trying to say you don't want me to go with you?"

I gasped. "What? No. I was thinking I should find another place to stay. I mean, being here feels slightly awkward."

"Do you have anywhere in mind?" he asked.

"Not really, but there's probably an inn on Moonstone Beach with vacancies. I could stay in one until I find somewhere else."

Cru shook his head. "No inns. I've got a place."

I laughed. "First a job. Now a place to stay. What's next, Cru? Are you going to find me a husband so everyone gets off my back about Beau?"

He opened his mouth as if to speak, but closed it.

"It was a joke. And apparently, not a funny one," I muttered under my breath when he stalked off down the hallway.

"Daphne!" Alex shouted when Cru and I walked into Stave. She came out from behind the bar and hugged me. "How are you?" she whispered.

"I'm fine," I said, pulling away and trying to figure out if she was asking about my ordeal in New York City or about Beau and Sam. "Hungry and thirsty, though," I said with a tense smile.

"Your usual?" she asked.

I didn't have one, but I supposed whenever I came in with Beau, I had a glass of whatever they were pouring from Barrett Family Vintners.

"Do you have anything open from Los Cab?"

Alex smiled. "Always."

She pulled an unmarked bottle out and poured three glasses.

"What's this?" Cru asked when he joined us at the bar.

"Taste and see," said Alex, who'd put the bottle away when she saw him approach.

I watched as he swirled, sniffed, and sipped, rolling the wine around in his mouth before swallowing.

He set the glass down and smiled. "Have you tasted?" he asked.

"I was too fascinated, watching you."

His eyes blazed, sending heat straight through me. God, didn't this man have any idea how fucking sexy he was?

My eyes opened wide and my cheeks flushed when something occurred to me. I didn't remember ever seeing Cru with women outside of the Wicked Winemakers bachelor auction every year, which I was sure Alex—the chair of the event—had roped him into doing.

No doubt, the bidders hoped the date they purchased would turn into something more. I guess it never had.

I'd always bid on Beau, mainly because he didn't want to have to go on a date with a stranger. The only person who'd ever offered more was his mum, saying the only way she'd get to spend time with her busy sons was through an auction date. It was so sad to think about now, knowing she wouldn't be there this year. She'd passed away suddenly on Christmas Day.

"Daph?"

I looked up at Cru, then at the glass I'd been excessively swirling.

"What are you thinking about?" Alex asked, wriggling her eyebrows.

"Oh, um, nothing, really," I responded before inhaling what was in the glass. I sipped, buying some time to think of an answer other than Beau's dead mother or wondering why I'd never seen Cru with a date.

Could he be gay? I'd never gotten that vibe from him, not that it would've bothered me if I had. Or maybe it would've, at least on a personal level. I'd been so hot for the man for so long that knowing he'd never be interested in me would be like letting go of a dream.

On the other hand, I supposed I could take solace in knowing that was why he'd never made a move—or at least one more reason he hadn't. That I'd been his best friend's girlfriend for so long was likely the primary factor. Then again, maybe he wasn't gay and my dating Beau didn't keep him from asking me out. Instead, he just wasn't interested.

"Well?" he asked after I'd taken a second sip.

"Um, it's good. Very good, in fact." The truth was my mind was so preoccupied with him that I hadn't been thinking about the wine at all.

When he looked crestfallen, I swirled again, inhaled deeper, then had another taste. This time, I let the wine linger on my palate. It wasn't just good; it was fabulous.

"Brilliant!" I exclaimed, taking another hefty pull from the glass.

His tense shoulders dropped, and he leaned his elbow on the bar. "You had me worried."

"I apologize. I was preoccupied, and I should've waited to taste. It really is fantastic, Cru. It's one of yours, isn't it?"

He leaned closer. "Maybe sometime I'll tell you what I named it."

I wanted to rest my head against his and breathe in the scent of him rather than the wine. More, I wanted to touch his lips with mine. Given there was at least a thirty-three-percent chance he was gay, another thirty-three-percent chance that my having been with Beau had turned him off, and a thirty-four percent chance he simply wasn't interested, I leaned in the opposite direction, reaching for the tapas menu.

I drank more of the wine while pretending to study the list of food. "What would you like?" I asked, handing it to him.

His eyes blazed a second time. "It isn't on the menu."

"Hmm," I said, wishing Alex hadn't walked away to help other customers. "That's a shame."

Cru nodded and took another sip, but his eyes never left mine.

I either needed to retreat to the ladies' room and douse my body with cold water or change the subject.

"So, um, I guess I should've asked if there was someone else you'd rather take to dinner tonight."

His head cocked. "Why?"

"Err, I don't know. Maybe there's someone special in your life who might get the wrong idea about me going with you."

"Everyone knows we're friends," he snapped, turning away from me to look around the crowded room. "Would you excuse me for a minute? I see someone I need to speak with."

"Of course," I said, staring into my glass, knowing my flush of embarrassment had traveled up my neck to my cheeks. Thankfully, he was too focused on whoever he had to talk to that he wasn't paying the slightest bit of attention to me.

I turned the stool slightly to see where he went. "Who's that?" I asked when Alex returned.

"You mean the guy Cru is talking to?"

"Yes."

She fanned her face. "*Muy caliente*, right?"

I nodded.

"That's Anthony Ricci. I'm surprised you haven't met him. I'm sorry to say he's happily taken, though, by another winemaker." She wriggled her brows.

I watched as the two men talked, both laughing at something Cru said. When Anthony reached up as if to touch him, I quickly turned away. It was bad enough thinking about the two men together. I didn't need to see it.

"Are you okay?" Alex asked again. This time, her eyes bored into mine.

"Yeah. Just feeling sorry for myself. More so, knowing Anthony's taken." I winked and smiled, hoping she bought it.

"There are a few other, single, heterosexual guys here tonight. I'd be happy to make an introduction if any of them interest you."

"Daphne has plans tonight. She's having dinner with me."

My eyes opened wide because I hadn't heard Cru return. Alex's did too, probably more from his tone of voice.

She looked from her brother to me. "Daphne, are you leaving town anytime soon?"

"She isn't," Cru snapped.

Alex put her hand on her hip. "I was talking to Daphne, who I know can speak for herself since she just asked me if Anthony Ricci was available."

I choked on the wine I'd just sipped.

"Are you okay?" Cru asked, patting me on the back.

"I'm fine," I said, grabbing a bar napkin to wipe my mouth. "Just tired of people asking me that," I added under my breath.

"Anyway, what I was going to say is, just because Daphne is having dinner with you this evening, it doesn't mean she can't do the same with someone else tomorrow night."

Cru glared at her. "Knock it off, Al."

She shrugged at him, then looked at me. "Did you decide on something to eat?"

I turned the menu that was face down over and pointed. "That." I took a closer look. "Spanish, err, octopus."

Alex made a face. "Really?"

"If it isn't good, why is it on your menu?"

"You're right. It's fabulous. Cru, what about you?"

"Bring us an order of roasted beets and beef tartare."

Alex cleared her throat.

"Please," he added.

"We won't be hungry for dinner," I commented when she walked away.

"Sure we will, considering you won't eat a single bite of octopus."

I folded my arms. "What makes you say that?"

"Read it."

I picked up the menu. He was right. Serrano chili oil and smoked paprika. One, I was allergic to, and the other, I didn't care for. I looked around for Alex, but didn't see her.

"Want me to cancel the order?" he asked.

"Would you, please?"

He stepped around the bar and walked in the direction of the kitchen.

"How did you know?" I asked when he returned.

"Las Golondrinas."

"Wow. What was I? Maybe sixteen?"

"Seventeen, and Beau ate a pepper, then dared you to do the same thing."

My eyes opened wide. "That's right. His was super mild, but he gave me the hot one."

Cru nodded. "Dickhead," he muttered.

I laughed. "And the paprika?"

"We were at somebody's house." He looked off into the distance, then shook his head. "I can't remember her name. Anyway, her grandmother made dinner for everyone, and whatever it was had paprika in it."

"I had hives all over my body." I looked up at him. "You called your mum, and she came to the house with allergy medicine. That was nice of you, Cru." I reached out to touch his hand, but he moved it away.

I took another sip of wine, then squared my shoulders. "Look—"

"I'm sorry. It's just that—"

I slid off the stool, reached into my bag, and pulled a couple of twenties out, then threw them on the bar. "I'm pretty tired. I think I'll pass on dinner. Please thank Brix for the invitation."

He stood too. "Wait. What? No. I, uh, wanted you to see the house."

"The house?" I shook my head. What had I missed?

"Remember, I said I had a place where you could stay? I'm buying Brix's house."

My eyes scrunched, and I gripped the back of the stool. "I think the wine went straight to my head. To be honest, I have no idea what you're talking about."

"Just come to dinner with me. We'll make it an early night. I promise."

"I still need to find a place to stay. It'll be easier to do it now. If I wait, there might not be any vacancies."

He shook his head and leaned closer. "I'm not leaving you alone, Daph. Whoever the guy was who locked you in that fucking room is still out there. What if he comes back?"

I hardly needed the reminder. The nightmares were bad enough. "I suppose I can return to Seahorse." I rolled my shoulders. "You know what's a better idea? I'll stay there tonight and, in the morning, catch a flight home."

Cru stepped closer. "Come to dinner with me. We'll figure the rest out later."

"Okay."

He leaned down to look into my eyes. "Did you say okay?"

I smiled. "I did."

"There's something I need to say," I began when we were in the car on our way to Brix's place.

He glanced over at me. "Go ahead."

"You're a good friend, Cru. I don't want to do anything to ruin that."

"Yeah, me neither."

I waited, but he didn't say anything else. He also didn't look over at me for several minutes.

3

Cru

"You need to stop acting like the best friend, so Daphne can see you as the leading lady—err, man." While the reference Brix had made to be the leading lady was weird as fuck, the rest of what he said resonated. Stop acting like the best friend. But how? Especially since she'd just said she didn't want to do anything to ruin our friendship.

Did she mean by working for Los Cab? To me, it was the perfect solution. Or was it staying in Brix's house? Which I guess wouldn't be his; it would be mine. I hadn't addressed either subject other than with a quick mention. Maybe I should.

"So, about the job, I'll be taking over the first label and am looking for someone to oversee the second. Since sales of the primary varietals are what bring in the most income, I've used the secondary to experiment with different blends and fermentation processes. What you tasted earlier was an example of what I consider a success."

"As you should."

I couldn't look over at her. The friend comment still stung.

"You'd have a lot of freedom to experiment."

"Cru, you don't have to do this."

I sighed and gazed out the side window at the curves of the hillside illuminated by the lights from the sparse houses. The drive from Cambria to Paso Robles was one of my favorites—day or night.

"Actually, I do. I can't make both."

"I'm sure there are other—"

"Daphne, you're looking for a job; I'm looking for a winemaker. If you aren't interested in working for Los Cab, or if it's working with me that is giving you pause, just fucking say so." My tone was harsher than I'd intended, but her hesitation was pissing me off. I saw it as the perfect solution.

"I would appreciate the opportunity very much."

Her voice was soft, which made me feel worse about the way I'd snapped at her. "I'm sorry."

"Apology accepted. You mentioned you wanted me to see the house?"

"You know how crazy it can get, depending on the time of year. Living on the ranch makes it easier, even if it isn't full time. Brix's place is huge. From what I remember, there are five bedrooms. Maybe six. If you stayed there, you wouldn't even have to see me if you didn't want to."

I glanced over at her, but her arms were folded and she wasn't looking in my direction.

"Or not," I muttered.

She sighed. "Why even say that? Is there some problem I'm unaware of? You asked me to just *fucking* say it if I didn't want to work with you. Why are you making these offers if you don't want to?"

She was right. I sounded like I was hoping she'd turn me down. Meanwhile, it was my fear—my insecurity—giving her an easy out. "Look, can we start over?"

"Sure."

I cleared my throat. "Daphne, there's a job opening at Los Cab for a second-label winemaker."

"I'm interested."

"It comes with an optional place on the ranch to stay rent free."

"Rent free?"

I looked over at her and smiled. "It's the friends-and-family discount."

"I'm interested in that as well."

"Great. It's settled. Now, we just need to get Brix and Addy to move out."

Daph chuckled, and I did too.

I breathed a sigh of relief that things were back to normal between us, but the ache in my chest remained. Normal was the last thing I wanted. Had I just confirmed friendship was the only thing between us?

"Come on in," said Brix, opening the front door and motioning us inside. "Addy's got dinner just about ready."

"Aren't you helping?" I asked.

"I was until she kicked me out of the kitchen. Apparently, having my arms around her is some kind of distraction." Brix looked over at Daphne. "Hey, I'm sorry for what I said this afternoon."

She nodded. "Apology accepted."

"Appreciated. Can I pour you a glass of wine?"

"Please." Daphne pointed to the kitchen. "Okay if I say hi to Addy?"

Brix nodded. "She'd love it."

When my brother walked away, I followed.

"I'm interested in the house, after all. As soon as you're ready."

Brix raised a brow but smiled. "I'm glad you've had a change of heart. Timing is the reason we asked you to come over. We're leaving sooner than expected."

"When?" I asked.

"Tomorrow."

I raised a brow, too.

"We decided last night. Addison thinks we'll make better progress on the house if we're there, and I agree. As far as the vines are concerned, you don't need me for pruning, which is all we do at this time of the year. Actually, there isn't anything you need me for between now and harvest."

"Understood."

"So, about adding another winemaker, I was thinking you could—"

"It's already handled."

Brix handed me two glasses of wine. "Yeah?"

"Daphne will be taking over the second label."

He motioned with his head, and I followed him to where she stood waiting, looking out a window at the night sky.

"I hear congratulations are in order." Brix raised his glass at the same time I handed one to her. "Welcome to the Los Cab team."

"Thank you. I'm excited to have the opportunity," she said, taking a sip when Brix did.

Since I knew which wine he'd poured, I waited for her reaction. I was rewarded when she looked at me with wide eyes.

"Another of yours?" she asked.

"Yes and no," Brix answered before I could. "You can explain. I haven't seen my wife in almost five minutes, and you know how I get." He winked at Daphne before going into the kitchen.

"What did he mean?" she asked.

"The blend is one of my father's. We haven't released it since not long after he died. I'm bringing it back."

"It's first label, yes?"

"It is. It will be my first official release since taking over as winemaker."

"It's a spectacular offering."

"Thanks." I couldn't help but smile. Daph had no idea what her opinion meant to me, both personally and professionally. "Oh and, by the way, Brix and Addy are leaving for Mexico tomorrow."

Daphne's eyes widened. "That soon? Or wait, on holiday?"

I shook my head. "For good. I mean, I'm sure they'll visit. They're just moving out of the house." I held up one finger. "Be right back." I stuck my head in the kitchen. "Hey, Addy."

She looked over her shoulder. "Hi, Cru. Dinner will be another twenty minutes or so."

"Does that mean I have time to give Daph a quick tour?"

"Of course," said Brix. "You know the way."

"We have a few minutes before dinner, so I'll show you around," I said, leading Daphne to the staircase. "There are two bedrooms on the main floor and three more on the second level. I'm not sure, but I think there's one more on the third." When we reached the landing, I motioned to the right, where the sleeping areas I mentioned were located. "Each has its own bathroom."

Daphne stuck her head in. "Very nice."

We walked through the den to the opposite side. "This is a second master," I said, going through the doorway. "You could have your pick of this or the one downstairs. They're the same design. Actually, one is right above the other."

She walked over to a door leading outside. "What's this?" she asked.

I joined her and opened it.

Daphne gasped. "Wow, a sleeping porch. This is brilliant."

"Wanna check out the third level?" I asked.

"Of course."

When we did, I wished we hadn't. It was set up almost like an apartment, albeit without a dedicated entrance. There was a third master bedroom, with a full bath, a living room, and a small kitchen.

Daphne surveyed the space but didn't appear interested, thankfully.

"Shall we?" I asked, motioning to the stairs.

"This is interesting," she said, resting her hands on the half wall framing the open area that went from the main floor to the roof, where there was a skylight in the same shape.

"The house was constructed using Vastu design principles where the center is open."

"I noticed it on the first floor and wondered," she commented.

"I don't know that much about it. All the buildings on Uncle Tryst's ranch were built the same way."

"Very cool."

"Dinner's ready," Brix shouted up to us.

"On our way," I responded. "So, what do you think?" I asked as we made our way downstairs.

"It's an amazing house."

"Do you think you'd want to live in it?"

Daphne was in front of me, so I couldn't see her face or her reaction. When we reached the second-floor landing, she stopped. "Are you sure about this?"

My eyes scrunched. "Why wouldn't I be?"

"I might cramp your style. You know, if you wanted to have someone over."

I had no interest in anyone other than her, so it wouldn't be a problem for me. Would it be for her? "Is that what you're worried about? I mean, that I'll cramp yours?"

She shook her head. "The weirdly awkward conversation is back."

"It doesn't have to be. A simple no works."

She folded her arms and raised a brow. "Does it?"

"Yes, Daphne. Or rather, no. You won't be cramping my style."

"Neither will you."

Brix talked more about the house, as well as the one they were building in Mexico, over dinner. "Every time we visit, Tryst has added another room," he joked.

"That may be my fault," said Addy. "I would really miss this dining area."

It was off the kitchen and had garage doors made of glass panels that could be rolled up, making it an outdoor space, or left down like they were tonight, when the weather was chilly.

It was difficult for me to stop myself from gazing at Daphne. I could stare at her for hours, but when she closed her eyes and kept them shut, I couldn't look away. What was she thinking about? Beau? Some other guy? Why was it never me?

I could feel someone else watching me and turned toward my brother. He frowned and shook his head.

4

Daphne

I shut my eyes for what I intended to be a brief moment, imagining Cru and I sitting out here, enjoying a glass of wine in the evening. Maybe he'd reach over and touch my hand. Or invite me to join him on the sleeping porch upstairs. Perhaps we'd lie next to each other and he'd stroke my hair like he had after taking me to the emergency room in New York City. I thought about how it had felt when he held me in his arms the day he found me.

When my fantasy about Cru morphed into memories of the man who'd locked me in a room, I opened my eyes. Cru, Brix, and Addy were all staring at me.

"Sorry," I said without explanation. My plate was still half full of food, but I wasn't hungry. In fact, if I'd tried to eat more, I likely would've become nauseated. "Can I help?" I added when Addy stood to clear her plate and Brix's.

"Let us do it," said Cru when his brother stood.

"I don't mind enjoying such a nice evening," said Addy, sitting down. "I'm definitely going to miss this place," she murmured once the guys were inside.

"You could always stay."

"Have you been to Tryst's ranch?" she asked.

"I haven't."

"When you visit, you'll understand why Brix and I would rather be there, regardless of how much we'll miss it here."

"I've heard it's quite nice."

She nodded once. "It is. More than that, though. The best word I can use to describe it is magical."

I could say the same about being in this part of the world. I'd always been drawn to the Central Coast of California. While the wine regions in the northern part of the state were breathtaking in their ostentatiousness, I found those in Paso Robles to be more welcoming. Los Caballeros especially.

The Avila family had settled in the area in the seventeen hundreds. The winery buildings, which reflected the family's Spanish heritage, hadn't been constructed for another hundred years, but that was still old by California standards.

In comparison, the family who owned the property adjacent to this were of Scottish heritage and their structures looked as though they'd been brought over from the Highlands.

I stood and looked out to the vineyards, which were illuminated by the moon. Working here would be a dream, particularly since Cru was willing to let me be the primary winemaker for the second label. I'd have to prove myself, of course, but I was always up for a challenge. At least when it came to wine.

The challenge Cru represented as a man was a different story. I could handle the rejection, if it came to that, but letting go of the dream of him and me being together would be hard on my heart.

In hindsight, I should've ended things with Beau years ago. Our relationship wound up being more of a convenience than a love affair. If I had, would I have had a chance with Cru then? On the other hand, maybe he was the winemaker Anthony Ricci was happily taken with.

"What I'd give to know what you're thinking," he said.

"I'm going to love working here."

He smiled. "I hope so."

If he hadn't reacted so strangely when I attempted touching his hand at Stave, I'd hug him. Instead, I wrapped my arms around my own body. "When do I start?"

"Would tomorrow be too soon?"

"Not at all." I bit my lip, realizing I had very few items of clothing with me. The little I'd taken with me on my misguided cross-country trip was left behind when Cru had rushed me out of the apartment.

Maybe that was the moment when I realized how wrong Beau had always been for me and how right Cru could be.

"What's wrong?" Cru asked.

"I don't suppose there are any all-night clothing stores anywhere nearby."

"I should've thought of that earlier today. I'm sorry."

I couldn't help it; I released my arms and touched his with my hand. "It wasn't your responsibility. I should've thought of it."

He looked down at where my fingers rested on his bare skin but didn't pull away.

"Does this bother you?" I asked.

"Why would it?"

"Earlier, it seemed like it did."

Cru removed my hand but embraced me. "We're going to make great wine together, Cullen."

"Speaking of Cullen, my parents are probably frantic with worry." I'd spoken with them from the hospital, explained I was there under an abundance of caution on Cru's part, then said I'd ring them the following day. It had been over twenty-four hours, and I still hadn't called. Since it was midmorning in Perth, I could get in touch now, but I didn't feel up to the conversation.

Cru dropped his arms, and his face fell. "I forgot to tell you. They're on their way. In fact, they should be landing soon."

"Where?"

"LAX, but they're catching a flight in the morning to San Luis Obispo."

"Bloody hell," I said under my breath.

"Sorry, Daph."

I shook my head. "Don't be. It isn't as if I don't want to see my mum and dad. I just know they'll try to convince me to return to Australia with them."

"Are you sure that wouldn't be a good idea?"

I looked at him and smirked. "You're trying to get rid of me already, even before we negotiate my salary?"

While he laughed, his eyes appeared more concerned than amused.

"Seriously, Cru. If you've had a change of heart—"

He put his finger on my lips to silence me, and all I could think of was how much I wanted him to kiss me instead.

"Let's make a deal," he said.

"All right."

"If I decide I don't want you here, or you decide you don't want to be here, let's agree to just say it outright. No more second-guessing. Like you said on the drive over, we're friends."

"You're right. So, um, my parents are on their way?"

He nodded.

"Is it terrible of me to wish they were arriving tonight, only because then I could stay with them rather than return to Seahorse?"

He chuckled. "Not terrible at all. However, you still don't have to. We can stay here."

My eyes widened. "I wouldn't want to impose."

"Not here, here. You can stay in the guest cottage. Or the main house—my mom would love it if you did."

"What about you?"

"I, uh, actually live in the guest cottage, which hasn't been used as one for a few years now."

"Good thing I didn't say that's where I'd prefer to stay."

"My mom would be just as happy if I stayed with her."

"My parents' arrival means I won't be able to start work tomorrow."

He shook his head. "Not even one day on the job, and you're already taking time off."

"Believe me, I'd rather be here."

"Come on. Let's take a walk."

"What about Brix and Addy?"

"He said she was tired and they were going to bed. I'll need to come over in the morning to see them off. In fact, I'm taking them to the airport. You might as well ride along and meet up with your parents."

"Good thinking." While I said the words, I didn't mean them. The longer I could put off the inevitable conversation about my return to Australia, the better.

"This is the cottage," Cru said after we'd been walking for several minutes. It had a white picket fence surrounding it and a lovely front porch.

"It's charming," I commented when he opened the gate and led me up the walk to the front steps.

"Fortunately, it was cleaned today, or I might be afraid to invite you in."

"Messy, are you? That surprises me."

He shook his head. "I left in a hurry the last time I was here. Beau, uh, needed my help."

He opened the door, switched on the lights, and motioned for me to come inside.

"You don't have to tiptoe around mentioning him. I already told you I'm not upset about him and Sam. I actually knew they were together before the rest of you did."

The color left his face. "That's right. You saw them in Vegas."

"You don't have to tiptoe around that subject either. I'm not afraid to talk about it. Actually, the more I do, the less horrific it'll seem."

"Glass of port?" he asked.

"I'd love one." I smiled when I saw he'd pulled out a tawny bottle. I preferred it over the traditional style.

We both sat on the sofa, and he handed me a glass. Our fingers brushed, and my breath caught when I looked up at him. It was more than his classically exquisite looks that stopped my heart. His mere presence was so dynamic, so full of virility, that I wondered how I'd ever managed to form words when I was around him.

He caught me studying him, and his gaze held mine as if questioning why my cheeks were flush and my palms so sweaty.

When I looked away, it was as though an invisible string tying us together snapped, and Cru's expression turned somber.

"You haven't said much about what happened."

I rested against the cushion. The police who took my statement wouldn't allow Cru in the room with me. After telling them what happened, I hadn't felt up to repeating it. Out of everyone, Cru deserved to hear the story the most, but he hadn't pressured me to tell him. The hardest part was having to admit how reckless I'd been.

"I met Ryder and two of his friends—a couple—at the airport in Los Angeles. They were headed to Las Vegas like I was, except I'd planned to catch a connecting flight from there to Nashville. We ended up seated next to one another on the plane, and they talked me into waylaying my trip and spending an evening in Vegas with them. Since I had no real plans in Nashville other than that I was bored and had never been, I took them up on their offer."

I looked into his eyes, expecting to see disappointment or something akin to it. Instead, Cru gazed at me with an understanding I'd never known with anyone other than him. Even my parents.

I told him that, coincidentally, the group was staying in a hotel my father had invested in on the strip. I booked my own room and met up with them later for a night on the town.

"Beau has a stake in that place, doesn't he?" Cru asked.

"Yes, so I suppose I shouldn't have been surprised when I ran into him and Sam on our way to dinner, but I was. Did you know he was there?"

He shook his head. "I didn't have any idea until he called me a couple of days later, saying he was in a small town outside of Buffalo."

"He wasn't exactly happy to see me." I could hardly blame my impetuous behavior in the days that followed on him. However, his attitude toward me that night had certainly fueled it. It still hurt when I thought about how rude he'd been when all I said was I was sorry to hear about his mum. It was like he couldn't get away from me fast enough. Maybe because he was with Sam. Like everyone else, did he think I was *butthurt* about it? I was really starting to hate that term.

Too ashamed to look at Cru while I recounted the next part, I studied the wine in my glass. "After far too much partying, I agreed to travel to New York City with them. I told you two of the three were a couple. I'm sure Ryder expected we'd hook up, but I wasn't interested in sleeping with him. He was good-natured about it when I turned down his advances. He even understood when I booked a room at a hotel rather than stay in the apartment he and his friends had let."

I took a sip of the wine, followed by a deep breath. "The next night, the four of us were out for dinner, and by the time it was over, I wasn't feeling well. I went to the ladies' room, and when I came out, I overheard them mention my parents. They said they were worth billions. It was then I realized the dizziness and confusion I was feeling was likely brought on by something they'd put in my drink."

Cru shifted closer. "You don't have to go on if you don't want to."

"I'd rather get it all out."

He nodded. "Go ahead."

"I returned to the ladies' room and called the first person I thought of—Beau. I was able to tell him I was in trouble, but not much else before I heard the restroom door open. Fearing it was Janine, the other woman, I ended the call. I don't remember anything after that until I woke up in a strange place and found the bedroom door locked from the opposite side when I tried to exit it. It wasn't long before you arrived."

"Thank God you're okay," he said, barely above a whisper.

When I looked over at him, my eyes filled with tears. "I don't deserve you."

"What does that mean?"

"Most people would tell me how stupid what I did was and that I'm lucky to be alive."

"Who among us hasn't done something crazy in our lifetime? As you're aware, I've had my share of experiences I wish I hadn't. Most of which you know about."

"The majority of them were with Beau."

He nodded. "Yeah, but there were a few others I was on my own."

"Thanks for trying to make me feel better, but mine is seriously worse than all of yours combined."

Cru rested against the cushion like I was and looked up at the ceiling. "There's one you don't know about."

I glanced over at him.

"I almost cost Los Cab our bond, which meant our license."

I hadn't heard anything about this, and if they had lost it, it might have cost their family millions.

In order to legally make and sell wine, wineries had to take out bond coverage, which served as an insurance policy required by the ATB, which covered a winery's annual excise-tax liability.

Calculating that tax liability wasn't an easy thing to do. It was based on the total volume, in gallons, that was stored on their site during any given month of the year. To further complicate things, that total volume had to be broken out by tax class, which was determined by each wine's alcohol content.

If a winery vastly underestimated their production, or if what they produced was significantly different in terms of alcohol content and they didn't bring their bond up to meet the changes, they could face stiff fines and penalties, including the loss of their license to sell the wine they produced.

"What happened?" I asked.

"I was way off in my estimates."

"I thought there was a grace period to correct miscalculations."

"There is." When he looked away, I could feel his shame.

I put my hand on his arm. "Tell me the rest."

"I moved the wine off the property and hid it. It was a stupid fucking move. It's just that Brix was different then. He was on my ass about everything. Not just mine, everyone's." He shook his head. "Still, he's not the one who did it. I am, and I had to face the consequences. Before I could come clean, someone moved the wine from the caves where I'd stored it, back to Los Cab. And, coincidentally, the ATB showed up about fifteen minutes later."

I shook my head like he had. "Damn, Cru."

"Right?"

"You said *almost* cost Los Cab the bond. What happened instead?"

"I'm not exactly sure who went to bat for us with the ATB, but I have my suspicions. There was a fine, but that was about all. At least from them. For a while, I thought Brix would fire me."

"Could he? I mean it's your family's business, not his alone."

"You're right, but he could make my life such a living hell until I quit."

"Is that what he did?"

"In the beginning, but then he backed off. I think the same person who stood up for us with the ATB convinced him to lay off me."

I pulled on the sleeve of his shirt so he'd look at me. When he did, I smiled. "Whoever this guardian angel is, I'd like to have him in my corner."

"I believe you have your own guardian angel."

"You're right. I know I do."

"Yeah?"

I nodded. "You're it, Cru. It wasn't just what happened in New York. You've come to my rescue more times than I can count. You've let me cry on your shoulder and given me a kick in the arse when I needed it. I mean, jeez, Cru, tonight you gave me a job and a place to stay."

His eyes bored into mine. "I'm not finding you a husband, though. Let's get that straight right now."

5

Cru

It had been bad enough watching Daphne and Beau together. I couldn't go down that road with her and another man who wasn't me, and I sure as hell wouldn't play matchmaker.

"It's late. Should I stay with your mum?"

"You can stay here." I stood. "The bedroom is in the back."

Daphne's eyes were wide. "You do know I was joking about finding me a husband."

"Of course I did." I scrubbed my face. "I'm tired." Not that it explained why I was suddenly being such an asshole.

"If it wouldn't be horribly inconvenient, given I don't have a car, I'd stay elsewhere—"

"Don't do that," I snapped. "We agreed."

"I didn't agree to put up with your surliness." She folded her arms. "I've never known you to be so moody."

If only I could pull her into my arms, stroke her cheek with my fingertip, apologize, and kiss her, all would be right with my world. Instead, I was being an asshole. "I'm sorry."

"I have to admit I don't understand. Is it something I've done?"

What could I say? That I was being a douche because I couldn't stand the idea of her with another man? Or that being near her turned me on so much I'd had to leave the room so she didn't notice how my erection strained against my jeans? Or that I couldn't remember the last time I'd had sex, yet the idea of being with anyone but her not only turned me off, but made me sick to my stomach? I couldn't say any of those things. Worse would be if I acted on the intense desire I felt for her.

Instead of doing one of the things I knew would result in me losing her friendship, I was doing the other.

"I'm sorry," I repeated, putting my hands in my pockets to stop myself from reaching for her.

"You haven't answered my question."

"I'm out of sorts, and as I said, I'm tired. While I know what you went through was horrific, as you said, I was still crazy with worry, terrified that something had happened to you. The idea that…" My voice clogged with emotion, and I couldn't go on.

Daphne stepped closer and, when she couldn't get me to take my hands from my pockets, wound her arms around my waist. "Why won't you hug me?" she whispered.

I sighed and embraced her. "I was so afraid I'd lose you."

Daphne rested her head on my chest. "Thank you for finding me. For saving me."

"You had to know I would."

I felt her nod. "I don't know why I didn't call you."

"It doesn't matter. You're here, you're safe, and that's all I care about."

She removed her arms from around me and took a step back. "We should get some rest."

I led her to the bedroom and showed her where I kept extra pillows, blankets, and towels.

"I just remembered my bag is in your car."

"I'll go get it."

"There's no need if you have a spare toothbrush."

I pointed to a couple still in their packages, along with unopened toothpaste.

"There are shirts in the drawer if you need something to sleep in."

"I'm good. I'm more comfortable not wearing anything to bed."

I swallowed the groan that came so close to escaping my lips. "Uh, good night, then." I backed out of the room and was about to close the door when I heard Daphne say my name.

"Yeah?"

"Thank you for everything."

I nodded once. "You're welcome. Anything else?"

"Should I meet you at the main house in the morning?"

"I'll come back."

She cocked her head but didn't say anything, so I closed the door.

While I'd told her I'd sleep there, I had no intention of doing so. If I had my way, Daphne and I would sleep under the same roof, even if not in the same bed, for as long as she'd allow it. Frankly, I'd prefer to never let her out of my sight.

When I woke the next morning, my body ached from sleeping on the small sofa and my cock was rock-hard from dreaming about Daphne naked in my bed. And instead of where I was now, in my fantasies, I was with her.

"Cru?"

I jumped when I heard her say my name, then shifted to an upright position while also attempting to keep the lower half of my body covered by the blanket.

"Good morning," I said, scrubbing my face with my hand.

"I thought you were staying at your mum's."

"Changed my mind." I glanced over and saw her in one of my sweatshirts. It hung down almost to her knees. Could my imagination have given me a break rather than conjuring the image of her naked beneath it? Then, naturally, picturing her bare pussy. Not that I knew, or would ever know, if she kept it that way. I grabbed a pillow and put it on my lap.

"You're a coffee drinker, right?" she asked.

"Yeah. If you give me a minute, I can make some."

"I'll do it. Where do you keep everything?"

"Beans are in the cabinet above."

When she opened it and reached up to grab the bag, the sweatshirt rose with her, almost to the top of her thighs. A gentleman might have looked away. Clearly, I wasn't one.

"This place is set up for a tall person," she grumbled. "Can you help?"

"Uh, sure." I really had no fucking idea what I'd do now. There was literally no way for me to hide my raging hard-on. So I stood up, and when I did, Daphne's eyes went straight to the tent in my sweatpants. Rather than look away, she *didn't*.

With the most confident swagger I could muster, I joined her in the kitchen, stood right beside her, reached up, and grabbed the coffee beans. I turned to face her, but her eyes were still riveted to just below my waist.

"If you keep staring at it, it'll probably get bigger."

Her eyes opened wide, and when she finally looked up at me, we both laughed.

"I'd say I'm sorry, but I'm not." She giggled. "Quite impressive, Cru."

"I call it morning wood."

She giggled some more.

"Keep laughing at it, and it will go away."

She put her hand over her mouth, not that it helped. "We wouldn't want that, now, *would* we?"

"You're hysterical. Make your coffee."

"I can't reach the cups."

I raised a brow. They were almost right in front of her face. In order for me to get them, I'd have to reach across her, and when I did, my body would press against hers.

"I'm gonna take a shower. Probably a cold one. If you can't figure out how to get a cup, I guess you'll have to wait."

"Hang on."

I turned to face her. "What?"

She wiggled her finger at my midsection. "Can you leave that here?"

I chuckled, shook my head, and went in the direction of the bathroom. "I haven't figured out how to get back at you yet, but know it's coming," I said behind me. Which, of course, was met with more giggles.

When I heard a knock on the door, then it opening, I wished there was a lock on it. I was hidden behind a shower curtain but still.

"Daphne? What are you up to now?"

"Coffee delivery. Would you like me to hand it to you or leave it on the counter?"

"Counter, please, and just remember, payback is a bitch."

"I'm looking forward to it."

I could just imagine the smirk that came along with her challenge. This playfulness, her teasing, was just one of the reasons I loved her so much it hurt.

If only she weren't yanking my chain, I would've returned to the kitchen, picked her up, set her naked butt on the counter, dropped my sweatpants, and fucked her senseless.

Instead, I was alone in the shower, taking care of my mad desire for her the way I always did.

"Are your parents staying at Norman?" I asked on the drive to the airport.

"I'm not certain, but it's where they usually stay."

There was a guesthouse on a vineyard owned by friends of Daphne's parents—George and Lana Norman—that I knew had two bedrooms. I just hoped she'd opt to sleep at Brix's with me tonight instead of there with them.

It dawned on me that, as of today, it was no longer my brother's house. He'd quit claimed the deed to me earlier, before we left. Maybe once I moved out of the cottage where Daphne and I had spent last night, I'd start referring to the bigger house as my place. Although I'd much prefer it to be Daphne's and mine.

I hadn't offered her one of the ranch vehicles to drive yet, since none of them would've been suitable to pick up her parents. The other reason I hadn't was because I wanted to be with her if they chose not to wait to question her about what had happened in New York City. It wouldn't be my business to defend her, but at least I'd be there to lend my support if it was needed.

Saying goodbye to Brix and Addy was harder than I'd expected it to be. Both made me promise to visit and to bring Daphne with me. Given I'd already thought about showing her Tryst's ranch, I said I would.

I hung back when Daph approached her parents, but she quickly led them over to me. I'd known Noah and Beatrice Cullen all my life. The man was still as fit as me. Only the wrinkled lines of his face gave away his age. It was the same with Daphne's mother. She was just as gorgeous as her daughter, with the same wide smile and warm eyes.

Daph's dad had been a good friend of my father's as well as a member of a secret society at the same time he was, like I was now.

The organization—known as Los Caballeros—was a brotherhood dating back several hundred years. My ancestors established the branch in the US when they came to the country in the seventeen hundreds; at the same time, they gave the name to our family's winery.

Like me, my brothers, and my dad, Noah's father and grandfather had been members. It was rare for someone who didn't already have a family connection to be asked to join, but if they were, they had to meet certain criteria.

First, they had to be presented for consideration by an active member. Next, their family had to have been in the wine industry for at least two generations. Third, the prospective member had to be worth a billion dollars or more in their own right. And lastly, they had to agree not to divulge the existence of Los Caballeros and the work we did to anyone outside of our tight-knit circle.

While not a mandate, having a good seat in the saddle was necessary, given the annual one-hundred-mile ride out we did in the spring—a Spanish tradition stemming back to the fourteen hundreds. It was then that the Knights Templar defeated the Moors and took control of a town, Jerez, in southwestern Spain. They renamed it Jerez de los Caballeros—direct translation: Jerez of the Knights.

Back then, the Templars' ride outs were more for marauding, whereas ours were about celebrating our ancestry and our love of traversing the desert into the mountains of Paso Robles on horseback.

The *caballeros* served another purpose. Some called us good-guy vigilantes. Law enforcement wasn't always thrilled with our involvement, but many had confessed—off the record—that our "interference" was appreciated.

When Addy was charged with murder a few months ago, we were the ones to prove her innocence and also to track down the real killer.

When Daphne called Beau to say she was in danger, he'd immediately rallied his fellow *caballeros*—through me—to find her. As had become the case in the last few years, we were aided by a private security and intelligence firm called the Invincibles, which was headed up by a man named Decker Ashford.

It wasn't the only firm of that nature we worked with. Another, K19 Security Solutions, was founded by the eldest son of the family who owned the vineyard estate adjacent to ours.

"Cru, it's good to see you," said Noah, approaching and embracing me. Daphne's mother did the same after hugging her daughter. "Daph tells me she has news about your winery."

I raised a brow in her direction, then winked. "Yeah, what is it?"

Her eyes scrunched at me when I didn't take the cue to tell them about her new job.

"I'm the second-label winemaker," she said. "As of today." Her cheeks flushed.

Noah's head cocked.

"You just missed Brix. He and Addy plan to live in Mexico permanently, so I'll be taking over the first label."

I was puzzled when Beatrice glanced at her husband and he nodded.

"Shall we?" I asked, motioning in the direction of baggage claim.

"By the way, the Normans are out of town and offered the use of their vehicle so we won't need to rent one," Noah said when we passed the car counters.

"I'll need to buy a car myself if I'm going to be living here permanently," Daph murmured.

"We can help with that while we're here if you'd like," said Beatrice.

While the conversation was seemingly mundane, what had just occurred wasn't. Daphne had stated she'd be remaining in the States, and by way of offering to help with a car purchase, her mother had communicated she was in support of the decision.

When Daphne and her mom walked away arm in arm, Noah hung back.

"I want you to know Bea and I enthusiastically support this new development."

"I'm happy to hear that, sir. Daphne will be a huge asset to the Los Caballeros brand. I'm excited to see what she does with the second label."

"Not that development, son."

"Sorry, I'm not following."

"You and our daughter. While we love Beau and consider him part of our family, Daph's mother and I always thought you'd be a better match."

"Wait." I stopped walking and put my hand on his arm. "It isn't like that. Daphne and I aren't together."

Noah's head cocked a second time. "You're not?"

My mind raced with anything she or I might've said that led them to believe we were a couple. I couldn't come up with a single thing. "Positive. We're friends. Nothing beyond that."

He shook his head and chuckled. "I wasn't born yesterday, Cru. You can't hide how much you love her, nor can she try to cover her feelings for you."

I'd argue the point more, but why? I'd not convince him otherwise. Besides, I did love her. The only thing he was mistaken about was his daughter's feelings for me.

6

Daphne

"I absolutely adore you and Cru together. It's about time, I might add."

My mouth gaped. "What are you talking about?"

My mum's brow furrowed, then she smiled. "There's no reason to hide it from your father and me. We approve, darling. Not that you need us to. You're a grown woman, able to make your own decisions."

My parents had always supported me, and they weren't game players. If they had been manipulative in the past, I might've wondered if that was a back-handed compliment.

"Recent errors in judgment notwithstanding," I muttered.

"Daphne, please do not say such a thing." She turned to face me and put her hands on my shoulders. "Nothing *you* did resulted in what happened in New York City. You were a victim."

"You don't know what occurred."

She pulled me into an embrace. "Of course we do. Your father spoke with Laird Butler."

My eyes opened wide. "How does he know?"

"Decker Ashford, one of the men responsible for finding you, told him. The two are quite close, you know. Laird, who is known as Burns in those circles, mentored him when he was a teenager."

I blinked several times and shook my head. "I have no idea what you're talking about. I do know Mr. Ashford helped locate me, but beyond that, you might as well be speaking a foreign language."

She cupped my cheek. "No matter. You're safe, and that's all we care about. We appreciated Cru's call, suggesting we catch the next flight out."

I glanced over to where he and my dad chatted. He appeared as confused as I was. "You don't think Dad would say anything to Cru about us being a couple, do you?"

My mum shrugged. "It wouldn't surprise me."

"No!" I gasped. I turned my back to the two men and put my hands on my flushed cheeks. "I'm telling you; it isn't like that between us. In fact, I think he might be gay."

She gasped. "Gay?"

"Shh." I pulled her farther away.

"Sweetheart, Cru is not gay," she said in a lower tone of voice.

"Have you ever seen him with a woman? Meaning someone he was involved with?"

She thought it over for a minute. "I guess I haven't. That doesn't mean he's gay, though, Daph."

I shrugged. "It also doesn't mean he's not."

She shook her head and put her arm through mine like she had earlier. "Come on. Let's see if our bags have arrived."

The ride from the airport to the Norman estate was quiet. I knew Cru well enough to pick up on his tension. Even if I didn't, the way he clenched his jaw would've been a clue.

"I'm sorry," I mouthed when he glanced over at me. That he shook his head only worried me more.

"I always love staying here." My mum sighed when Cru pulled through the gates and we drove past the vineyards I'd visited so many times when I was growing up.

I often wondered why my parents hadn't invested in vineyard property on the Central Coast, but now that

I was an adult, I understood they couldn't spend too much time away from the businesses in Australia.

"It is beautiful," I commented. "Not on par with Los Caballeros, though."

Cru glanced over at me a second time, still not smiling.

"I'm not just saying that. It's always been my favorite."

Finally, he smiled. "Mine too."

From the corner of my eye, I saw my parents glance at each other. I had no doubt the look was meant to affirm they were right about Cru and me. Even though they weren't.

The conversation he and I would have to have later would be awkward and embarrassing, but I had to reassure him that I hadn't done or said anything to make them believe we were a couple.

"Can we take the two of you to dinner tonight?" my father asked when Cru pulled up and parked near the guesthouse.

"I'm sure Cru is busy—"

"I'm not."

"Oh, um…" I hadn't expected him to interrupt me. "Well, then, it would be lovely. Thanks." I turned to face my mother. "I need to do a bit of shopping this afternoon if you'd like to join me."

"Could we do it tomorrow instead, sweetheart? I hoped to take a nap before dinner. You know how dreadful the flight over is."

"Sure. Of course." I'd need work clothes before tomorrow, but I'd figure something out.

"I'll take you," Cru offered quietly.

We made sure my parents were settled, then left them to rest. As soon as we were back in the SUV, I took a deep breath, then turned to him.

"I want you to know I didn't say anything to lead my parents to believe you and I were anything more than friends." My cheeks flamed in embarrassment.

"Neither did I."

"I don't know where they got the crazy idea…"

Cru nudged me with his elbow. "Wishful thinking. Your dad told me he'd always liked me better than Beau."

When he smiled and winked, the tension in my shoulders released.

"Who wouldn't?" I said, winking back at him.

"Where to?" he asked once we were out on the highway.

"It's a bit of a drive, as well as in the direction from where we've just come, but I think San Luis Obispo might have better options."

"I don't mind. Slow time in the vineyard, so we might as well take advantage of it. I don't know about you, but I don't think I can wait until dinner to eat."

I put my hand on my rumbling tummy. "Me either."

Rather than head south, Cru drove out to Moonstone Beach and parked in front of the Olallieberry Diner.

"I love this place."

He nodded. "More to love about it now. My ma and Addy's are running it."

"How wonderful!"

"You don't know the half of it. Ma hardly has time to get on her kids' cases anymore."

"I'll admit I love that about her."

Cru chuckled. "That's because it gives you more to give me shit about."

"You don't know the half of it," I repeated.

"Brat," he muttered, getting out of the SUV. "I wish you'd wait for me," he said when I climbed out before he came around and opened my door.

I rolled my eyes. "Sorry, but I am perfectly capable of getting it myself."

"What you aren't capable of is allowing me to be a gentleman."

As I walked past him, he swatted my bottom and I playfully yelped. If anything, I wished he'd be far less of a gentleman and do more of what he had earlier this morning when he didn't even try to hide his erection. I had such fun when we teased each other.

"Is that what will happen if I do something wrong in the vineyard?" I batted my eyelashes.

"If I say it will, I'm afraid you'll cause problems intentionally."

"You know me too well."

"Enzo!" Cru's mother shouted his given name when we walked in the diner's front door. "I knew you'd come see your mama this morning." She pretend pouted. "I miss my Gabriel and Addy already." I'd only heard Cru's oldest brother referred to as Brix for so long that I almost forgot his real name. "Daphne, it is so nice to see you too, sweetheart," she said to me, holding out her hand.

"You'll be seeing a lot of her, Ma. Starting tomorrow, she'll be working at Los Cab."

His mother, Lucia, clapped her hands. "In the tasting room?"

Cru put his arm around her shoulders. "No, in the winery. She'll be taking over the second label."

Lucia's eyes opened wide. "She will?"

"Yes, and she'll be making fabulous wine."

His mother tried to smile, but it didn't come through her eyes. "That will be nice."

"Sorry about that," Cru said when we took a seat at the farthest table from the kitchen.

"I take it she doesn't approve." When I rested my hand on the surface, he covered it with his.

"It isn't you. No one other than an Avila has ever made our wine."

"What about your brothers? None of them wanted to take it on?"

He shook his head. "Cristobal, as you know, is a doctor and lives in Palo Alto. Snapper and Kick are on the rodeo circuit, currently making bank. Brix is out of the picture, and Alex is busy with Maddox at their winery. That leaves Trevino."

"How is he?" I asked.

Cru pulled his hand from mine. "I worry about him. Ever since the accident…"

It wasn't really an accident. Two men were able to bypass Los Cab's security system and had not only kidnapped Addy's mother, who was staying on the ranch at the time, but they'd knocked out both Lucia and Trevino. What they'd done to Trev was far worse than him simply losing consciousness. While I didn't know for sure, I wondered if he'd suffered brain damage. "I'm sorry."

"I guess if you married one of my brothers, you'd count as an Avila."

He meant to tease, but his comment stung. How was he to know that the only brother I'd marry was him? Not that he'd ever want to marry me.

"Sorry," he muttered. "It was supposed to be a joke."

"I know," I said, picking up the menu and raising it high enough to hide my face.

"Daph?"

"What?" I asked without lowering it.

"Look at me."

"I thought you were hungry. Decide what you want to eat, so we can order."

When he didn't say anything else, I figured he'd done as I suggested. Instead, when I lowered the paper, he was still looking at me.

"It was a joke."

I glared at him. "I *know*. Would you drop it, please?"

"It's just that—"

"I was hoping I'd find the two of you here," said Alex, taking one of the empty chairs. She looked directly at me. "I was wondering if you'd be interested in managing Stave."

"She can't," Cru answered before I could. It wasn't the first time it had happened in the last couple of days, and it was starting to annoy me.

"Okay if I speak for myself, or is a second-label winemaker not allowed to talk?"

"Say what?" Alex jumped out of her chair and pulled me up too. "I'm so excited. Second label? That's fantastic!"

Alex's enthusiasm was dampened by Cru's scowl. Even after we sat down, he glowered.

"What the fuck, Enzo?" Alex said under her breath. Apparently, her use of his given name did nothing to diminish his irritation.

"Would you leave? No one invited you to join us for breakfast."

"Touchy, touchy. Well, I'm happy for you, Daph. If you decide not to work for the ogre, the job offer remains open."

Alex got up, but instead of walking out the door, she went into the kitchen.

"I'm sorry," Cru said as soon as she was gone.

I folded my arms on the table and leaned closer to him. "What is going on? You've apologized to me more in the last two days than in all the time I've known you."

"Things are different between us now."

I shook my head. "Only if we let them be. Look, if you've changed your mind about the job, I'll be disappointed, but I won't be angry. Same thing with staying in Brix's house. I can get a place on my own. I'm not strapped for cash, Cru."

"We're friends."

"As we both keep saying, and the best thing we can do is get ourselves back to that. You don't want to hire me? No problem, we'll still be friends. You don't want me living in your house? Again, no problem. We're friends."

"Can we *please* just drop it?"

"Sure."

"What can I get you for breakfast?" asked a waitress I didn't recognize.

"I'll have a side of dry toast, please."

"Wheat, rye, sourdough, white, pumpernickel, or whole grain?"

"Whole grain, please."

"Is that all you're gonna have?" Cru asked.

"I'm not that hungry."

"How about you, Cru? Should I get your regular order, sugar?" The waitress smiled and winked at him.

"Skip the toast. We're not staying," he snapped. At least I wasn't the only one he was doing it to.

He stood, and I did too.

"Will I see you later, sweetie?" she asked when we were almost out the door.

"I think she's talking to you, *sugar*."

"Knock it off, Daph."

I shook my head. I was on the verge of tears, and it took a lot to make me cry.

"I need some time away from you," I said. "I'm going back inside alone. I'll order what I really want for breakfast, then I'll either get a ride from Alex or ask my parents to pick me up."

"Can we please talk?"

"That isn't working. I need some time. I'm asking nicely, so please give it to me."

He hung his head. "Sure, but you have to promise me you'll stay with Alex or your parents."

"Thanks."

"No, not thanks. Promise me you won't leave here with anyone but them, and when you do, Alex either brings you to Los Cab or to Norman, and that's only if your mom and dad are there."

"I promise."

I had my hand on the diner's door when I heard him say, "Will I see you later?"

"Probably, *sweetie.*"

"What was that all about?" Alex asked when I sat at the same table and Cru drove off.

"To tell you the truth, I have no bloody idea. Things have been off between us, and I don't know how to get back to where we've always been—friends."

"Did you sleep with him?"

My mouth gaped, and while I wanted to yell, I lowered my voice instead. "*No. God!* How could you even ask me that?"

"Want some coffee?"

"Yes, please. I also want food, but I'd rather not order it from Cru's girlfriend." If she was his girlfriend. I still couldn't decide whether or not he was gay.

Alex looked around the room until she spotted the woman I was referring to. "Her? They were never together. I'm sure she wanted to be, but he wasn't interested."

The woman was certainly attractive and very much into him. Again, I couldn't stop myself from wondering if his lack of interest in women was because he preferred men.

Alex set the coffee in front of me. "What do you want to eat?"

"An olallieberry muffin, warm please."

"Is that all?"

"For now, thanks."

She went into the kitchen while I prayed the waitress wasn't carrying a sharp knife that might end up in my back when she passed by.

"I got it, hon," Alex said to her, setting the muffin in front of me like she had the coffee. She sat down and leaned closer. "You have nothing to worry about with her. Even if they were ever together, I'm sure she wasn't more than a hookup."

"Wait. I'm not worried about her, other than her stabbing me," I added under my breath. "I don't care who Cru hooks up with."

She nodded but with her head cocked.

"Cru and I are *friends*. Not only that, but he's my boss. At least, I think he is."

She plucked a piece of my muffin. "That's the problem with you two. Too much sexual tension."

"You're not even listening to me." When she went for another piece of my breakfast, I slapped her hand. "Get your own."

"I should. I like peach better, anyway." She got up and left again, but returned empty-handed in under a minute.

"Out of peach?" I asked.

"Nah. I decided to have something else. My ma is making us both breakfast."

I studied Alex. Maybe it wasn't just Cru whose mind seemed to race in a hundred directions at once. Maybe all the Avilas acted like he did, and I'd just never noticed.

"Okay, so anyway. Cru is crazy about you, and from what I've seen, the feeling is mutual."

"I love your brother, but not in a romantic way. He feels exactly the same." I leaned closer. "And what about Anthony Ricci?"

Her eyes scrunched, then opened wide. "Oh my God! Did you think I meant Anthony and Cru were together?"

I shrugged. "Since I've never seen him with a woman, I thought maybe, you know."

Alex laughed out loud. "The reason you haven't is because he's been hung up on you since the first time you met." She looked at my plate. "Can I have some more while we're waiting? I'm starving."

I pushed the plate in front of her.

"Wanna bet?"

"About what?" I asked.

"How Cru feels about you."

I shook my head. "At the moment, I'd rather not know."

"Just leave it to me," said Alex at the same time her mother delivered breakfast, which looked like enough food to feed all seven Avila siblings.

7

Cru

There were two ways to get to Brix's house. One went through the back, and not many people knew about it. Since there was someone right behind me, I kept going and pulled through the main gates.

This way would go by the winery buildings and the main residence. Ma wouldn't give me grief for not stopping in; she was at the diner.

When I got close, I saw someone else sitting on the porch. So I pulled off the drive and parked.

"Hey, Bit. Nice to see you." My dad had been the one to give Trevino the nickname. At the time, he'd called him Little Bit, since he was so much smaller than the rest of us. Even Snapper and Kick, who were two and three years younger than him, were taller by the time Trevino was ten. He eventually shot up in height and filled out enough to be on the offensive line when he played high school football.

"Where's Ma?" he asked.

"At the diner."

My brother nodded.

"Do you need something?"

"Thinking about breakfast." He'd always been a guy of few words. I couldn't say whether his head injury had made it worse or not.

"I haven't eaten if you wanna go with me."

He stood, walked down the porch steps, and I followed.

"Where's your car?" I asked after we were in mine.

"Parked by the caves."

I cringed. The caves were where Trevino was attacked, and it was where he always went first when he came on the property.

Once on the road, I drove in the opposite direction of Moonstone Beach and headed into the historic part of Paso Robles. My gut ached and my shoulders were tense ever since I left Daphne at the diner. I was supposed to be watching over her, protecting her, and keeping her safe. I just prayed she kept her promise and stayed with my sister or her parents.

"Joe's or Cowgirl's?" I asked once I found a place in town to park. Either one was fine with me. They both had good food, although neither was as good as the Olallieberry Diner.

"Cowgirl's," said Trev.

"Dad liked Joe's better," he mentioned when we walked into the other place.

"Was Cowgirl's even open before he died?"

He shrugged. "Probably not."

We were seated and had ordered breakfast when I told Trevino that Brix and Addy had left that morning.

"He messaged, and I saw them earlier."

"I'm really glad, Bit."

He nodded. "I hung out with Snapper and Kick a couple of weeks ago too. They won big at NFR."

"Cool." I hadn't even known that. National Finals Rodeo took place in mid-December. I saw my two youngest brothers at Christmas, and they hadn't mentioned how they did.

"I saw Cris too."

"Sounds like you're making the rounds, bro. Anything up?"

"I'm leaving California." His words were like a punch to my gut, unless he was headed to Mexico.

"Where to?" I asked.

"Don't know yet."

"Have you seen Uncle Tryst?"

"Might go there first."

The waitress brought our food faster than it seemed they could cook it.

"You should, Bit. I'm sure Brix could use some help on his house."

He didn't say much else until he finished eating. "Brix said you're bringing Daphne on to take over the second label."

"That's right."

Trevino pulled out his wallet, threw some cash on the table, and stood.

"Ready to go?" I asked.

"If you are."

I wasn't, but I could get the rest of my food to go. I signaled the waitress, who brought a box over.

We drove to the ranch in silence. I figured my brother had said everything he wanted to already and didn't press for more.

"Do you want me to drop you at the caves, or are you sticking around?"

"Are you moving out of the guest cottage?"

I glanced over at him. "I am. Why?"

"Could I move in?"

"Of course you can, Bit."

"Cool. Maybe I'll stick around a while longer, then."

Trev had never been interested in making wine, or I'd have asked him if he wanted a job too. "I can take you there now if you'd like."

When he nodded, I turned the SUV around.

"I have clothes to pack up and some other personal stuff, but everything else comes with the place."

He turned in a circle in the living room once we were inside. "Was Daphne here last night?"

"She was. It was late, so rather than finding another place to stay, she bunked here." I pointed to the pillow and blanket on the sofa. "I slept there."

Trevino nodded. "You should marry her."

"Yeah?"

"You two are perfect together."

"Thanks, Bit. I think so too. I'm not sure Daphne feels the same way, though."

He shrugged. "You'll never know if you don't ask."

Trevino and I got all my stuff packed and looked around to see if Daphne had left anything behind. I'd gotten her bag out of the SUV before we left for the airport. After she showered and changed, she'd packed it up and I took it back out, figuring we'd drop it off at Brix's place later.

I chuckled.

"What's funny?" Trevino asked.

"I'm buying Brix's house. I guess at some point, I need to figure out something else to call it."

"Casa Del Sol."

I thought it over for a minute. "It's perfect." I'd always consider the house warm and welcoming. "Thanks, Bit."

"You should follow all my advice." He glanced over his shoulder and smiled.

"You got that right, brother."

"Where to?" Trevino asked when we carried my stuff inside.

The one thing Daphne and I still had to figure out was who would sleep where. I had a feeling she'd want the bedroom on the second floor since she appeared enamored with the sleeping porch. For now, I'd unpack my stuff in the one on the main level, which was directly below the one she'd be in.

"In there," I said, pointing in that direction.

"Got it," said Trev. He brought half the stuff into the bedroom, then went out to get more.

I sat on the bed, wondering why I was here and Daphne wasn't. How had things gone wrong so quickly? Not to mention, I'd vowed not to leave her alone, and that's exactly what I'd done.

Still need more time? said the message I sent.

Good on time. Now, I need clothes. Yours are all too big for me, she responded.

I nearly wept with relief. While things would continue to be awkward as we got used to being around each other, we were going to be okay.

Where are you? I asked.

Outside.

I rushed over to the front door and saw her sitting on the porch swing, laughing with my brother. All I could think as I watched them was how I wished every day could have moments like this. Having Trevino home felt so good. That I'd wake up every day knowing I'd see Daphne, felt even better.

"Hey, guys," I said, walking out to join them.

"Daphne needs wellies, jeans, and sweatshirts."

"Yeah, Bit? Is that all?"

He looked up at me and smiled. "I'll let you figure the rest out." He got off the swing and walked off the steps.

"Where are you going?"

He thought for a minute. "Shit. I gave you the good name. I'll have to think of something else for the cottage."

"How about Casa de la Luna?"

He laughed out loud. "Or Casa de la Luna…tic."

My brother never seemed more like his old self again as he did while walking away. I loved him so damn much and worried about him constantly. I just prayed he'd decide to stay here instead of taking off to wherever he was thinking about going earlier.

"I forgot you call him Bit," said Daphne. "It certainly doesn't fit him now. I mean, I like it. It's just that out of all your brothers, Trevino is the most, err, muscular."

"Thanks a lot," I joked. "I'm about the only one he lets get away with calling him that." I studied her. "We good?"

"Better than."

"Wanna go shop?"

"Have you eaten?" she asked.

"Yeah, um, I've got half a breakfast burrito left if you want it."

She shook her head. "Your mum made a traditional Avila breakfast, and while it was just for Alex and me, she doesn't know how to cook for fewer than seven people."

"Think you'll be hungry again for dinner with your parents?"

"If I walk enough of it off while we shop." She winked.

God, I loved her. All it took was her smile to remind me how much I did.

We spent all afternoon in downtown San Luis Obispo, shopping for clothes for her and me. I knew I'd love everything I bought, only because Daphne picked it out.

Between each store, I took the bags and put them in the SUV.

"What are you doing?" she asked when I waited outside rather than follow her into a store called Fanny Wrappers. Based on the window displays, they didn't carry men's underwear.

"I'll stay out here."

Daph shook her head and wiggled her finger. "Get in here, *Enzo*. I need your opinion." She held up a pink lace bra. "This or that?" She pointed to a peach-colored one in the same design.

I pictured the thin material covering the generous curves of her breasts. Her frame was slight but powerful, with defined muscles honed by years of running, surfing, and walking miles and miles of vineyards.

Knowing that if I didn't turn away, imagining her wearing anything they sold in this store would give me a raging hard-on, I looked out the window rather than at her. "Both."

"What about purple?"

"Yep."

"Black?" she asked.

"Every color of the rainbow. Although black isn't one of them. Every color they have."

"There are matching thongs too."

My eyes rolled back in my head as I imagined the thin, colored lace peeking out between the cheeks of her pert, hard ass.

I glanced over my shoulder at her and saw she was covering her mouth, trying not to laugh.

"You are such a brat."

Daphne giggled, took my hand, and led me to another part of the store where she plucked a garter belt from a display table and held it up. "What about this?"

It was sheer with navy flowers. "Fuck me," I said under my breath.

Daphne raised a brow.

"That means yes. You should get it."

"I think I'll wear it." She carried her armload of purchases to the checkout counter but held up the garter belt. "Would you mind if I wear this after I've paid?" Daphne motioned to a fitting room.

"Have at it, honey," the woman said, looking me up and down. "I know I would."

Between her shenanigans this morning and this, she had a *helluva* lot of payback heading her way.

8

Daphne

Alex had said to leave it to her to find out how Cru felt about me. That in itself was worrying. One never knew what Alex Avila-Butler might have up her sleeve.

He definitely reacted to my lingerie teasing. But would he think I was just being playful, or a brat, as he'd called me? Or would he realize how hard I was flirting with him?

"What time is dinner?" Cru asked once we were in his vehicle and headed out of San Luis Obispo.

"Typically at eight, but let me check. Their body clocks will be wonky." I sent my mum a text, then looked over to find him studying me.

"How's the lingerie?"

I wiggled my bum. "Interesting."

"Not the word I expected you to use."

My face scrunched, and Cru laughed.

"What?" he asked.

"It might be TMI."

"Suddenly, that's stopping you?"

"It's just that my skirt isn't quite long enough to cover my bum when I'm seated."

"And?"

"I should've thought to wear knickers."

Cru glanced at my lap, groaned, and put his eyes back on the road.

"You asked, and I did warn you."

"Lesson learned."

I reached over and touched the sleeve of the pull-over he'd put on over his shirt. "I like this."

"Good thing since you picked it out."

"Do you not like it?"

"I love it, Daph." He looked down at my legs. "And I love the stockings."

I ran my hand down my thigh and wriggled my eyebrows. "They're silk."

"One would think you're intentionally trying to drive me crazy."

I batted my eyelashes. "Crazy how?"

"I'm a man, Daphne, not a robot." He didn't even attempt discretion when he adjusted his trousers.

"Do you have the same reaction with all your friends?"

Cru rested his elbow on the arm of his seat and looked out at the perfect view we had of the ocean from the highway. "Here's the deal, my *friend*. We're going to be living and working together, side by side, every day. At night, I'll be in the bedroom right below yours. There's a lot at stake here, Daphne."

I had to turn away so he wouldn't see how humiliated his words made me feel. Truly, it wasn't his fault. I was the one playing games, as he'd said. I'd started it yesterday, and today, I took it farther than I should have. "You're right, and I'm sorry, Cru."

"I think we should dial it back."

"You mean I should."

He shook his head. "If that's what I meant, it's what I would've said."

"It was nice to see Trevino today." I hoped we could get off the subject of my blatant attempt at seducing him, especially given he clearly wasn't interested in me.

"He said he was leaving California, but when he heard I wasn't living in the cottage anymore, he changed his mind. I wish there was something in the winery he liked to do."

"There's *nothing*? I mean, there are so many options."

He shook his head. "If there is, he hasn't found it yet."

My phone vibrated, and I looked down at my mum's response. "She asked if we'd mind eating a bit earlier."

"I'm good with it. When?"

"Thirty minutes?"

"Where?" he asked.

"The Sea Chest. She said they want to enjoy the view before it gets dark."

"We should be able to make it on time."

I remained quiet the rest of the drive, still humiliated that Cru had called me out on my behavior. Something occurred to me, and depending on his answer, I might have to find another place to live.

"What's the rule about bringing dates to the house?"

His hand was tight on the steering wheel, and his jaw clenched. "Do you mean to spend the night?"

"Yes."

"I don't think it's a good idea. What about you?"

"I don't, either."

Cru turned his head toward the ocean again. "I don't want things to be awkward between us, Daph."

"I've already apologized, but I'll say it again any-way. I'm sorry."

"I wish I knew how to get us back to where we used to be."

I blinked away tears, hating that was all he wanted, but knowing it was for the best. "So, the waitress, is that someone you're dating?"

His brow furrowed when he looked over at me. "Are you sure this is a conversation you want to have?"

"You're right. I don't. What time do you want to start tomorrow?"

"I try to be in either the winery or the vineyard by nine at this time of year."

"Have you finished pruning?" I asked.

"Not everything."

I hoped he'd let me help tomorrow, but if he didn't, I'd understand. For now, I'd happily be the equivalent of an apprentice. The opportunity Cru had given me was exactly what I'd been looking for, and what had I done? Flirted with him shamelessly and made him uncomfortable. From now on, things would remain professional between us. We could still be friends, just never anything more.

When we arrived at the Sea Chest, my parents were first in line.

"How long have you been here?" I asked when Cru dropped me off and went to park.

"Your mum insisted we get here no later than four so we'd have a better chance at getting a table."

"Looks like you'll have your pick."

The restaurant didn't accept reservations, so diners were seated first come, first served. Hence the line that formed outside every day they were open.

"Look at you guys at the front of the line," said Cru when he joined us. He shook my dad's hand and kissed my mum's cheek.

The three made small talk while I looked out at the Pacific Ocean. I loved it here on Moonstone Beach, and having the chance to work at Los Cab meant I'd be less than thirty miles from it. I should be counting my bloody blessings instead of doing my best to muck everything up.

Stormy, who ran the restaurant, seated us at the best table in the place. It was in the farthest right corner and had a panoramic view of the beach and ocean. This was why my parents got here so early. The table was my mum's favorite.

"Cru, would you like to do the honors?" My dad asked, handing him the wine list.

"Why don't we let Daphne pick?" he suggested instead.

I perused the options. There were so many of my favorites that I had a hard time choosing. Finally, I went with a Norman Chardonnay in honor of my parents' visit.

"I had an interesting conversation with Roan Norman this afternoon. You remember him, don't you, Daph?" my dad asked.

"Of course I do. Gosh, it has to be ten years or more since I last saw him. How is he?"

"He's taken over full production from his dad, which I suppose is one of the reasons George and Lana are traveling so much. He asked about you."

Roan Norman and I had gone on a couple of dates when Beau and I were on a break. He was a nice guy, but I honestly didn't remember having that much in common with him. At the time, I was twenty and he was twenty-four—one year younger than Cru and Beau. "I don't recall him having an interest in wine-making."

"He must've acquired one," said my mum, peering over her menu.

"Cru, do you know Roan?" my father asked.

"I do—"

"Did I hear my name? Or are you talking about another guy called Roan?"

I laughed, and so did my parents. Cru did not.

"Daphne, it's really good to see you."

"Likewise." He'd aged in the time since we dated but in a good way. The truth was, he could be a male model; that's how good-looking he was. He was tall, with a powerful build, like Cru's, but instead of dark, almost-black hair, Roan's was golden like the hillsides in the valley. And, rather than deep bourbon-colored eyes like the man's seated to my left, his were blue.

"Hey, Cru."

"Roan," he responded without looking up from the menu.

"When you said you were coming here tonight, I started craving their food. I'll let you enjoy your dinner. I've got a spot at the oyster bar."

"No, don't eat alone. Join us." My father motioned to the empty chair between my mum and me.

"I don't want to intrude." Roan looked between Cru and me.

"Did I mention Daphne is working for Los Caballeros?" my dad asked.

Roan raised a brow. "Really?"

It would've been a good time for Cru to chime in on the conversation, but he didn't.

"Have a seat, Roan," my dad said, pointing to the open chair a second time.

"If you're sure you don't mind."

"Not at all, do we, Daphne?" My mother leaned over and nudged me.

"Of course not."

Roan made his way around the table. It would've been easier had Cru stood to allow him to pass, but he was behaving as though he hadn't heard a single word of the conversation.

"Can I give your seat to someone else?" Stormy asked, approaching the table.

"Of course. Sorry. I should've come and told you," said Roan.

She waved her hand. "Not a problem. So, can I bring you anything to drink while you're waiting to order?"

"Two bottles of Norman Chardonnay, please," I said.

"Excellent. Will you be tasting, Daph?" she asked.

"Please."

"You didn't have to," said Roan, leaning into me.

"I actually chose it before you got here."

"Well, I'm honored, nonetheless."

My father engaged Cru in conversation while my mum and I chatted with Roan. Every so often, I'd glance in their direction, thankful Cru had livened up a little. I found my dad's about-face from earlier today intriguing. Then he and my mum had sounded as though they were ready to send out wedding invitations. Maybe whatever Cru had said to him about us while I was speaking with my mother convinced him we were nothing more than friends and never would be.

"Cru?" said my mother partway through our meal.

"Yes, Beatrice?" he responded, setting his utensils on the edge of his plate.

"Daphne said she'd be starting work tomorrow, but I was wondering if you could spare her one more day."

"Mum!"

Cru put his hand on my arm, and warmth spread throughout my body. "It's okay. I'm sure your parents want to spend time with you."

How could I tell him I'd rather be with him, err, be at work without hurting my mother's and father's feelings?

"I was hoping you could stay with us, and tomorrow we could have breakfast together," my mum added.

"Of course I can do that," I said when Cru removed his hand.

Not only had I bought clothes and boots today, I'd also picked up a few extra personal items like shampoo and a toothbrush, so it wasn't like I'd have to get my bag from Los Cab.

"I can drive you over," Cru said as we were leaving the table.

"No need. I've got my car, and I'm going that way anyway," said Roan, who I hadn't seen approach.

"It is out of your way," I offered when Cru appeared to be waiting for an answer.

"Right. Makes more sense for you to ride with your parents."

I didn't miss his *suggestion*. "I'll have to get a few of my things out of your SUV."

We all walked out together, and Roan told my mum and dad we'd be right behind them.

"Hang on," I said. "I have some things I want to put in your trunk."

Dad popped it, and Cru and I started moving the bags over.

"Oh, wait, not all of that is mine," I said when I saw Roan pick up the rest.

He set them down and put his hands in his pockets.

"I think that's all," I said to Cru. "Thanks for taking me shopping today."

He leaned in close to me. "It was my pleasure."

If I hadn't resolved to stop flirting with him, I might've wriggled my eyebrows or attempted a witty comeback. Instead, I nodded once, closed the trunk, and got in the backseat when Cru opened the door for me.

"I guess I'll see you sometime tomorrow, then?" I asked.

"Take all the time you need. The job will be there when you're ready to take it."

My heart hurt when he walked away without saying anything else.

9

Cru

I kept my mouth shut for most of dinner, mainly because I feared if I didn't, I'd say something I'd regret when jealousy spread through me like a poison. Roan Norman was a douchebag, but Daphne was smart enough to figure that out herself.

As I had before, I took the front entrance into the estate. The main house was dark, which wasn't unusual. My ma got up at four every day to get to the diner, so she went to bed early.

The lights were on in the cottage, though, and since I could see Trevino sitting on the porch, I stopped.

"Where's Daphne?" he asked when I walked up the steps.

"With her parents."

"I thought she was staying with you."

I shook my head. "Her parents haven't seen her since everything went down in New York City, so I get why they'd want to now."

Trevino studied me. "What went down?"

"Yeah, I forgot you didn't know."

After we went inside and he got us both a beer, I filled him in on the call she made to Beau and how we were able to locate her a few hours later.

"Think they were hoping for a ransom?" Trev asked.

"Since Daphne said she overheard them talking about her parents' wealth, yeah."

"Fucking sucks, man."

"You got that right, Bit."

"So where did you say she is now?" he asked.

"Her parents are staying in the guesthouse on the Norman vineyards. Roan joined us for dinner," I added.

"I don't like him."

I laughed. "Me neither."

I left shortly after that, unloaded the SUV, and took the bags to the bedroom. I planned to put it all away in the morning, but since I wasn't tired, I started unloading them. I picked the biggest one up and saw a Fanny Wrappers bag inside it.

"Shit," I muttered, setting it on the other side of the room, hoping I could forget it was there. I lasted less than fifteen minutes before walking over and pulling out the contents.

I unwrapped the tissue and saw a few of the bra and thong sets she'd purchased. It seemed like she'd gotten more than what I was looking at, so I hoped she had some others with her. Just in case she didn't, I sent a text.

Missing something?

I was about to ask if you had anything extra.

Do you need any of it tonight? I asked.

Why?

I shrugged. Not that she could see me. *I could bring it over.*

I'd say yes, but that hardly seems fair, she responded.

If you need it, you need it. I don't mind.

I watched the marching dots, waiting for her response. When it came over, I was surprised to see how short it was, considering the length of time it took her to write it.

I don't.

What were you going to say instead, Daph?

I kept my eye on the screen but didn't see anything indicating she was sending another message. I was about to set the phone down when it rang.

"Hey, Daphne. Everything okay?"

"I promised myself I wouldn't do this."

I sat down on the bed. "Do what?"

"I don't know how to be anything but myself, especially with you."

"Why do you feel like you can't be yourself?"

"I tease you."

"Yeah?"

"And I flirt."

"There's nothing wrong with either of those things, sweetheart."

"Earlier, you said…Never mind. You know what you said."

"If I hadn't, what would you do right now?"

"Tell you I miss you already," she whispered, but I could still hear her.

"I miss you too."

"Good night, Cru."

"Hey, Daph? Before you hang up…"

"What?"

"Can you please come home tomorrow?"

I couldn't see her, but I knew she was smiling.

"I can do that."

"Good."

I was in the vineyard, checking to see if anything else needed to be pruned, when I saw the car Daph's parents were driving the night before pull in through the gate. I walked toward the house when they parked in front of it.

Noah had almost unloaded everything by the time I reached them.

"I didn't expect you so early," I said, taking some of the bags from his hands.

"Daph didn't feel right about missing a full day of work."

I cocked my head. "She didn't have to worry about it. Now, I feel bad."

"Don't. Her mum and I raised her to have a strong work ethic. We shouldn't have asked her to stay with us last night. I don't think she got much sleep."

I looked up at her when Daphne came out the front door. When our eyes met, I saw what led to her dad's assumption. She didn't look like she'd slept at all.

"Let me get those," I said to Noah. He handed me the bags he'd been carrying, and I met her on the porch.

"Hey," I said when we were face-to-face.

"Hi, Cru."

I motioned for her to go back inside. "What's going on?"

Her eyes filled with tears, and I set the bags on the floor. "Daph?" I asked, pulling her into an embrace. "Talk to me."

She buried her face in my shoulder. "I couldn't sleep."

I stroked her hair like I had when we were waiting for her to be seen in the emergency room. "Why not?"

She shook her head.

I tightened my arms around her. "Just tell me."

"It was the first time since, you know, that you weren't with me."

I leaned back so I could see her face. "I should've thought of that."

"The nightmares…"

"I've got you, Daph," I said, continuing to stroke her hair.

"I'm sorry."

I shook my head. "You aren't allowed to say that anymore."

She half smiled. "No? What about you?"

"Neither of us."

She took a step back, and I dropped my arms. "I don't know why it was different last night than it was at the cottage. I thought you went to sleep at your mom's, which meant I thought I was alone."

"You knew I wouldn't leave you. You sensed I was still there."

She shrugged. "I guess."

"So, what do you say we spend some time getting settled in the house?"

"What about pruning?"

"Nothing is ready yet. I checked."

"I could unpack my clothes."

I nodded. "Wait here." I came back a few seconds later with the errant bag.

She peeked inside. "You opened it."

I held up both my hands after she took the bag. "I confess. I couldn't resist."

She tried to hide it, but I saw her smile.

We spent the rest of the morning and early afternoon reorganizing the kitchen. While we rearranged cupboards, we made a list of things that were missing or that we wanted our own of.

The other thing we decided was who would sleep in which room. It didn't take long for me to convince her to take the one with the sleeping porch once I reminded her about it.

Daphne wasn't as animated as she had been, but she also didn't seem as down as when we were at Seahorse.

"More shopping and a late lunch or maybe an early dinner?" I asked. "We could also cook here."

Her eyes opened wide. "Oh no."

"What?"

"I told Roan I'd meet him."

"We can do our stuff another day," I offered.

Daphne shook her head. "I don't want to."

I stepped closer, and as much as I wanted to touch her, I didn't. "If you want to meet him, I'll understand."

She folded her arms. "If the situations were reversed, I wouldn't."

"What do you mean?"

"Never mind."

Did I really need to make her say it? I'd noticed jealousy rear its head at the diner when Shelley flirted with me. It wasn't nearly as much as I felt when Roan couldn't take his eyes off Daphne at the Sea Chest. But it was all I could do not to get up and throw him through the front window.

"There. It's settled," she said, setting her phone down.

"What is?"

"I'll meet him another day."

"In that case, I have an idea," I said.

"Go on."

"We'd have enough time to shop for the household stuff on our list, swing by the market, then invite your parents for dinner."

Daphne's eyes opened wide, and her smile was broader than I'd seen since I found her in New York City. "I love that idea, Cru. What about Lucia and Trevino? Could we invite them too?"

"If you're up for it."

The timing was perfect if I could sneak Trevino away for a few minutes to talk to him about my ideas for the upstairs porch. I'd been thinking about it since she and I were out there and saw how taken she'd been with it.

"I'll ask my parents; you ask your mum and brother."

I watched as she sent a message. She laughed at either her mom's or dad's response, then quickly replied. All the while, I wondered if this was how our life would be if we took our relationship beyond friends. It was too soon, though. First, we had to see if we could work together. That was primary. It was

Daphne's dream to have her own label, to make her own wine, and it thrilled me to make it happen for her.

I wasn't selfless in wanting her to work for Los Cab, though. By hiring her, I had someone to take over the second label, allowing me to focus on our main varietals, plus my dad's blend that I was still perfecting.

When she'd tasted it at Stave, I told her that maybe sometime I'd tell her what I'd named it. My dad never had because he hadn't gotten it "exactly right," as he'd say. If he had, I knew he'd have named it for my mother, just like I'd named it for Daphne—the woman I loved with all my heart—enough to do everything in my power to make sure she remained in my life, even if she could never be in my bed.

10

Daphne

Last night, I shut my eyes and drifted to sleep only once. It seemed that, within minutes, I dreamed I was locked inside a room, unable to get out. Except, unlike at the apartment in New York, I wasn't alone in this one. Ryder was there with me. I shook myself awake, but after that, I was too afraid to close my eyes again.

Rather than risk sleeping, I got my tablet out and read a book until sunrise, then made coffee and waited for my parents to get up. In Australia, they were early risers. Who knew what timetable they might be on only one day after arriving in the States.

"Something smells good," my father said when he joined me in the kitchen a few minutes after the coffee finished brewing.

We sat in the breakfast nook, and he asked me about Cru. At first, I tried to play it off as nothing, but he saw through it.

I told him about the conversation we'd had and that Cru said there was too much at stake for us to experiment by adding romance to the mix. Those weren't his exact words, but I knew that's what he meant.

"We need time to let things happen naturally between us, Dad," I'd said. "If we force it, there's far more to lose than a romance. I might lose my job and, worse, one of the most important friendships of my life."

"He's a good man, Daph," he responded. "Most wouldn't care enough to handle it the way he is."

"Beau wouldn't have."

He nodded and rested his chin on his hand. "You and Beau had your time. If it was meant to be, you'd be with him."

I told him I agreed, and while everyone assumed I was devastated by his relationship with Sam, I wasn't. In fact, I was relieved. I wouldn't have turned my back on him after his mother's death—it hadn't even been a month yet since it happened—but I was glad he'd reached out to Sam instead.

I think Cru was right when he said I'd sensed he was in the cottage two nights ago. I couldn't say whether the reason I felt so safe with him was because he'd rescued me or because I'd felt that way for years.

He was always there for me when Beau wasn't. Even when he and I were on again rather than off. I hoped things were different between him and Sam—that he loved her enough to take care of her instead of expecting she'd always be the one to see to his every need. I didn't know Sam well, but based on the little I did, I couldn't see her being Beau's doormat.

Cru had always put me first, and after being stepped on so many times by Beau's metaphoric dirty shoes cleaned off on my rough exterior, I wondered if Cru felt the same way about me now. Did he look at me and wonder if I'd ever put him first? Had I ever? I was ashamed to think that, if I had, it wasn't as often as I should have.

"They're in," I said when he set his mobile down.

"My ma and Bit are too."

"This will be such fun. Do you have any ideas about what we should serve?"

"I haven't thought about it yet. Do you?" he asked.

"What would you think about sushi tacos? If raw fish is an issue, we could cook some of it. I was thinking salmon, tuna, and yellowtail. We could also substitute one of these for lobster. I'd make different salsas or sauces for each and use both raw and toasted nori."

Cru's eyes opened wide. "That sounds amazing. Are you sure it isn't too much work?"

"Hardly any at all, actually. It's just a matter of cutting up the fish, then making the salsa or sauce. Toasting the nori only takes a few seconds if we do it on the stove." I walked over to the cooktop and removed the griddle, exposing the grill side.

"I'm in. Just tell me how I can help."

"I'll need a ride to the market," I said, winking.

Rather than go north once we reached the coast, Cru went south, in the direction of San Luis Obispo. A few miles into the drive, he pulled off the highway onto a dirt road.

"Where are we going?" I asked.

"To the best wholesale fish supplier on the coast."

"I never knew this was here," I said when he parked in front of what looked like a shack.

Inside, though, was nothing like I'd imagined. While not on the same grand scale as the Sydney Fish Market, this was equally impressive. I took my time perusing the options.

"What do you think?" Cru asked.

I chuckled. "I could shop here every day. Everything looks so fresh."

"Not far down the road is another wholesale market that sells produce, and next door to that is a bakery."

"I can't believe Beau never brought me here." I regretted the words as soon as I said them, but Cru didn't appear fazed.

"He doesn't know about it."

"I'm surprised."

Cru chuckled. "I kept it a secret since I wanted to be the one who brought you here first."

I studied him when a man behind the counter initiated a conversation. Cru was hot as fuck, but he never acted like he knew he was. His arms strained against the fabric of his shirt in the same way his powerful thighs filled out his jeans. That, along with the mental picture I had of his hardness from yesterday morning, had me squeezing my legs together.

As if he sensed my gaze, Cru turned his head. His eyes met mine, then traveled to my hardened nipples that had nothing to do with the temperature inside the fish market. I didn't bother trying to mask my attraction—the desire I felt was far too powerful to hide.

"Hey, Daph. Come meet Captain Bob."

The man's skin was tan and weathered, but his hair had no gray, making it difficult to guess his age. "If I were ten years younger, you'd have competition for this beautiful woman."

"I've got plenty of it now," said Cru, putting his arm around my shoulders in the way he might if we were more than just friends, and I loved it so much I beamed up at him.

"Do you want to choose or let the captain?" he asked.

"If you don't mind," I said to the man who studied us.

"My pleasure. Cru said you want tuna, yellowtail, and salmon. He also said you'd be open to lobster in place of the sockeye."

"Yes, please."

Cru removed his arm but remained close as we waited. I brushed his hand with mine, wishing he'd hold it, but he didn't. As much as I yearned for him in this setting—a smelly, damp market with concrete floors—how would it be when we worked in the vineyards and the winery? The latter was equally damp and smelly, just of grapes rather than fish.

And what about when we were home after a long day of work, making the evening meal together after we'd both changed out of our work clothes and were fresh out of the shower? In the summer, I knew he'd wear shorts once we were home, like I probably would.

Cru leaned down so his mouth was near my ear. "What are you thinking about?" he whispered.

"Summer."

His head cocked.

"Don't ask," I whispered back.

His eyes blazed, and he nodded once. "I won't. At least not yet." His smirk told me he saw this as an opportunity to get back at me for teasingly torturing him the morning at the cottage and later in the lingerie store. Honestly, I couldn't wait to see what he'd do.

As it turned out, he didn't do anything, at least not on our way to the produce market, bakery, or kitchen supply store. I sat on pins and needles the entire return trip to Los Caballeros, then again after we took our purchases in and put them away. In fact, he hardly said one word to me. I was beginning to realize I didn't know Cru half as well as I thought I did.

Maybe his teasing and flirting, in all the years our paths crossed, he'd done because he knew I wouldn't take him seriously since I was with Beau. Now that he wasn't a barrier between us, Cru realized I might take his playful banter to mean more than it did.

The other thing that bothered me was how everyone assumed he and I were together. Didn't anyone think I was capable of being on my own? Did I always have to be linked to a man? Men certainly weren't defined by whoever they were dating or married to.

I prepped three kinds of salsa plus two types of sauce. Captain Bob had cooked the lobster tails while we waited and chopped it, the tuna, and yellowtail in the way I'd told him I'd serve it. The salad was prepped, and the dessert we'd purchased at the bakery would only need to be cut later. Besides plating and serving, I'd still have to air fry both the raw and toasted nori, but I wouldn't do that until we were almost ready to eat.

"Anything I can do?" Cru asked when he returned from the caves where he'd chosen a few wine options.

"Everything is set. I was wondering, do you still keep horses on the estate?"

"We have a full stable."

"Would it be possible for me to ride?" I asked.

"Of course. I'll change, and we can go," he offered.

"You don't have to join me if you don't want to."

His eyes scrunched. "I'd like to."

"Very well, then. I'll change and meet you outside in a few minutes."

"Daph?" he said as I walked away.

"Yes?"

"Is everything okay?"

I turned around and put one hand on my hip. "*Everything* is okay. *I'm* okay. There's no need to keep asking."

"Gotcha."

"How about you, Cru? Is everything okay?"

He smirked. "Yes, Daphne."

"Good." I spun around and raced up the stairs, realizing Cru was absolutely right in saying there was too much at risk for me to keep flirting with him. He and I were meant to be friends, but clearly, not lovers. It had only taken three days to come to that realization.

"I can tack my own horse," I said when Cru brought one out of the stall, then proceeded to brush him.

"I don't mind." He ran his hand over the animal's withers.

"What's his name?"

"This here is Goose."

I slowly approached, letting him make eye contact with me, then held out my hand to touch the bridge of his nose. When he didn't flinch, I stroked the same area, stepping closer every few seconds. When he bumped me with his head, I wrapped one arm around him and stroked his mane.

"He likes you," said Cru.

"It's all about building trust, which is why I'd rather take care of him myself."

"Sure. Makes sense." He handed me the brush.

Twenty minutes later, we were both ready to ride. Fifteen minutes after that, Cru pointed to an opening in the trees. "There's something I want to show you."

I nodded and followed. We led the horses through a shallow stream that would likely dry up by late spring.

"What is *that*?" I asked when I looked ahead of us and saw an abandoned building.

"The original winery."

We dismounted and tied the horses to a split-rail fence.

"Is it safe to go inside?" I asked.

"The building is sound, if that's what you're asking."

I raised a brow. "But?"

"Critters may have taken up residence."

Something occurred to me. "Cru, why don't you have a dog?"

He was about to open what looked like the main entrance, but turned around. "Sometimes, it seems like you can read my mind."

"Yeah? Have you been thinking about getting one?"

"I actually thought about it on the way back from the fish market. There's a rescue facility on the opposite side of the highway."

"You could've stopped."

Cru nodded. "I decided a new dog and hosting a dinner all in the same day might not be the best idea."

"We could go tomorrow. I mean, unless you want to go alone, in which case you can obviously go whenever you want to."

He studied me. "Why are you so nervous around me?"

I shrugged. "You said it yourself. Things are different between us. We don't have Beau as a buffer anymore."

When he sat down on a bench just outside the building's entrance, I sat beside him.

"I feel like I keep swinging and missing," he murmured.

I thought about his analogy. It was the perfect way of putting how I felt too. "My life has changed so much so quickly."

"I've been pushing you."

"You haven't. I mean, what would I have done without you? Two days ago, I had no idea what I might do with my life. I didn't even know what part of the world I'd live in. I hated the idea of leaving California, the Central Coast in particular. I had the dream of being a winemaker but had no idea how to make it a reality."

"Right place at the right time."

I'd been watching the horses, but turned to look at him. "You don't even know if I can do it."

Cru shook his head. "Your palate is impeccable."

"You just say that because I love your wine so much."

"Your education is the best there is. You've grown up in the business, but more, I've watched you in the vineyard. You don't just walk among the vines; you close your eyes and breathe them in. You look at the fruit as though you can see through the skin to the pulp. It's as if your mind knows the sugar content without needing a hydrometer. I've seen you run your hand over the graft union up the trunk as if you know exactly what that single plant needs. It's in your blood, Daphne. I just thank God I get to watch you create what I know will be pure magic."

My eyes filled with tears at his words. "You humble me," I whispered.

He shook his head, then stood and held out his hand. "I believe in you. Come on, let's go inside." When he pushed the door open and went first, I heard him gasp. "What the hell?"

There was a switch on the wall, and when I flicked it, lights all over the large room came on. "It's so beautiful."

"Hey, I thought I heard voices."

I grabbed Cru's arm out of reflex when Trevino came around a corner.

"Bit, did you do all this?" There was awe in Cru's voice, and for one of the very first times, I saw a truly genuine smile stretch across his brother's face.

"Just cleaned it up some."

Cru walked over and ran his hand over the top of a tasting bar. The base was made of the same stone as the building, but the top looked like the same kind of oak that grew on the property. "I'm stunned, Bit."

Trevino joined us at the bar. "I've always liked this room the best."

"I can't remember when I was in here the last time, but it wasn't very long ago. Maybe three weeks."

"Four."

Cru smiled at his brother. "Were you spying on me?"

Trevino shook his head. "Hiding."

I watched the man I loved more with every passing minute as he walked over and embraced his younger brother. "It's amazing, Bit."

"I was thinking you could do private tastings here. Maybe wine dinners since it's more intimate than the main building."

Cru turned to me. "I love that idea. What do you think, Daphne?"

I went behind the bar and opened one of the cabinets built into the stone. My eyes lit up when I saw it was stocked with glassware. "Is there anything here we could uncork?" I asked Trevino.

He came around to where I stood and opened a cabinet on the outer wall. "Take your pick."

"You choose."

He reached to the lowest-level rack and grabbed a bottle from the far right, handed it to me, then pulled out a somm's knife. "You do the honors."

I did and poured three glasses, raising mine. "Here's to the next generation of Avila wine-making gods." I clinked Trevino's glass, then Cru's.

If he and I were alone, I would've asked why his eyes bored into mine so intensely. Then, when Bit left the room, why Cru took his place behind the bar, put his hands on my waist, and lifted me to sit on it. The only thing stopping me from asking why he spread my legs and stood between them was my inability to form words. Then, when he cupped my face and leaned forward, I stopped breathing.

11

Cru

A mere hair's breadth separated my lips from Daphne's when my brother returned to the room and cleared his throat.

"Sorry, but, um, Ma's looking for you." He held up his phone.

I stepped out from between Daphne's legs, pulled my cell from my pocket, and saw I'd missed calls and messages from her.

"Hey, Ma," I said when she picked up.

"Enzo, where are you?"

"In the old winery building. What's up?"

"There's been an accident at Demetria. Maddox is being airlifted to the hospital."

Fuck. This wasn't good. "Do you know his condition?"

"I do not."

"Where's Alex?"

"With him."

"Okay, Ma. I've got this."

Looking at my brother's face, I knew our mother hadn't shared why she was trying to reach me. Rather than ask, he left the room.

"I've got to talk to Bit, then I need to get to the hospital," I said to Daphne. "Maddox is being airlifted as we speak."

"I can take care of the horses."

"It'll be faster if we ride them to the stables. One of the guys will get them cooled down."

"I can do that if it will help."

I squeezed Daphne's hand. "The biggest help I need from you right now is to go to the hospital with me. I'm sure Alex will appreciate it too."

"Of course."

I rushed off in search of my brother.

"Hey, Bit," I said when I found him in the rear storage area.

He turned away from me.

"There was an accident at Demetria. Maddox has been injured, and Alex is with him. They're headed to the hospital. We'll meet them there."

He faced me. "You don't need me."

"Maybe I don't, but Alex certainly does. Daphne and I are taking the horses to the stables, then we'll leave. Do you want to meet us at the house, or should I pick you up at the cottage?"

Trevino's eyes bored into mine. He had to know I wouldn't back down on wanting him to go with us.

"I'll meet you."

"Good. Let's go."

When I returned to the main room, I didn't see Daphne, but found her outside, already mounted up. She'd also untied my ride.

"Bit's going along," I said, throwing a leg over after she nodded.

On the way back, I thought about how I'd address my mother not telling Trevino about Maddox's accident. If I were him, I'd be just as hurt as he looked.

Truthfully, there was no reason for either Daphne or Bit to go with me to the hospital other than I wanted her with me, and my brother needed validation that he was an integral part of our family.

The other thing I'd need to address was the kiss she and I had almost shared. I'd spent most of my adult life fantasizing about Daphne. Of course I'd imagined what sex would be like, but my yearning was for things as simple as holding her hand, her head resting on my shoulder, and how it would feel when our mouths, lips, and tongues finally touched.

The times when she and Beau were "on again" were the worst. My best friend wasn't opposed to PDA, and there were only so many excuses I could come up with to walk away or find someone else to talk to so I didn't have to watch them together.

Still, I hadn't been able to keep myself from sneaking glances at them. It didn't matter that, each and every time, I felt like I was being ripped in two.

We rode up to the stables, and when I dismounted, I realized Daphne was studying me.

"Are you sure you don't want me to stick around here?" she asked.

"I want you with me, Daph."

We'd increased security on the ranch after what had happened with Trevino and my mother, but the scariest thing was how fail-safe we'd believed it already was then. I wanted Daphne to feel safe here, comfortable, so how could I explain that I had to be with her and keep her close enough that if she faced any kind of harm I could keep it from happening?

As we led the horses into the barn, I felt the weight of her unasked questions—things I knew we'd have to discuss soon. First, though, we needed to get to the hospital and find out what was happening with Maddox.

We were on our way out, headed to the house, when Trev pulled up. "I can drive," he offered. I opened the front passenger door for Daphne, unable to stop myself from leaning closer when she got in and taking in her scent. If only my ma had waited a few more seconds, I'd know her taste too.

Alex rushed over when we met her in the emergency room waiting area. "He broke three ribs and has a collapsed lung. They're removing the air from the pleural space now," she said.

"Have you spoken to Cristobal?" I asked. Our brother was a medical doctor but had chosen to go into genetic research rather than a traditional practice.

"Yes," she snapped.

I raised a brow. "And?"

"You know how he is. Cris said it isn't a big deal and they'll probably let him go tonight or tomorrow."

I pulled my sister into a hug. "What did the doctor say?"

"Same thing." Alex wiped her tears on my shirt—something she'd done since she was a kid.

"There isn't anything they can do for broken ribs," said Trevino. I hadn't realized he'd come in after insisting on letting Daphne and me out while he parked the car. "Not a lot for a collapsed lung either. The lung will repair itself once the extra air is out of the pleural area."

I released Alex, hoping she'd rush to our brother like she had with me.

"Trev, thank God you're here," she said, doing exactly as I'd prayed.

He embraced her tentatively at first, but when she tightened her hold, he did too.

I glanced around for Daphne and retreated in her direction when I saw her waiting a few feet behind him.

"Did you hear?" I asked.

"Collapsed lung and broken ribs," she murmured. "Your brother was right when he said Maddox would likely be released tonight or in the morning."

"Mrs. Butler?" I heard someone say from behind me. I looked over my shoulder and saw Alex had approached the nurse who'd said it.

"We're going to keep your husband here for a couple of hours to monitor his breathing," she said.

"When can I see him?"

"Right now," the woman responded.

Alex turned and looked between Trevino and me.

"Go ahead."

She held her index finger up to the nurse, then walked over to us.

"I appreciate you coming so much, but you don't have to stick around."

"You guys take my SUV. I'll stay here with Alex," said my brother.

My eyes met my sister's, and she nodded. "I'll be okay." She turned to Trevino. "They said one person can come back with me."

He handed me his key fob and followed my sister and the nurse.

"Ready?" I asked Daphne.

When she said she was, I led her out to the parking lot. Thankfully, Trevino's fob had a long range, and when I pressed the unlock button, it was easy to find where he'd left his vehicle.

"You're quiet," I said once we were in the car and on our way.

She shrugged a shoulder. "I didn't want to be in the way."

I reached over and squeezed her hand. "You never could be."

"Cru, about…"

I knew the question was coming. "I'm sorry. I never should've done what I did."

"What did you do?" she asked.

"The kiss."

She nodded once. "You're sorry."

Her words were so monotone I couldn't get a read on how she was feeling beyond her being upset. "I'm giving you mixed signals. On one hand, I say there's too much for us to lose if we become more than friends, and on the other—you know what happened."

"*Almost* happened."

"You're right. So, uh, thoughts about dinner?"

"I'd hate for all the fish to go to waste," she said without looking at me.

"Have you spoken to your parents?" I asked.

"I told them I'd give them an update after I knew more about Maddox's condition." Her hand was limp in mine, so I released it.

"Do you want to call them now?"

She shook her head. "I'll wait until we're at Los Cab." She raised her head. "Unless you want to drop me off at Norman. We're not that far."

"I doubt you'd trust me to finish making dinner without your assistance." I smiled and nudged her with my elbow.

She smiled too. "You'd manage."

"I doubt I could manage much without you by my side." The words were out there, and I couldn't take them back. It didn't matter that I'd just admitted I was giving her mixed signals.

"I think we need to talk, Cru."

"Okay."

"Not tonight."

"Daphne—"

"I said not tonight."

She'd rarely snapped at me, so when she did, I was stunned but also happy. The ability to be real with each other was something I also craved.

We'd just walked into the house when my cell rang with a call from Alex. "They're letting Mad out now. Bit mentioned something about dinner."

"Yeah, um, we'd planned to have Ma, him, and Daphne's parents over."

"Got room for two more?" she asked.

"Sure, if Maddox feels up to it."

"He's a bear, one who's feeling no pain, by the way, other than hunger pangs."

I hit mute on the call. "Okay if Alex and Maddox join us tonight?" I asked Daphne, who was pulling food out of the fridge. Her eyes widened. "Not at all if he feels well enough."

I told Alex they were more than welcome, then hung up. The same overwhelming feelings I'd had in the old tasting room returned full throttle. I had to clench my fists to stop myself from approaching Daphne, lifting her so she sat on the kitchen counter, and ravishing her mouth with mine. The need I felt was almost too powerful to ignore. Was it really necessary to fight my attraction to her as hard as I was?

I sensed her approach from behind me and tensed. If she got too close, I wouldn't have the willpower to keep my hands to myself. When she rested her palm on the center of my back, so many emotions flooded my system. I couldn't process all of them. Want, desire, relief, and connection, but most importantly, love.

"Cru?"

"Daph, if I turned around right now, I won't be able to resist—"

"Turn around, Enzo."

12

Daphne

His breath caught when I called him by his given name, and heat radiated from his body to mine through my palm. I'd reached the point where I didn't care what we had to lose. The attraction between us was too great to deny. Before, I'd wondered whether he was as into me as I was him, but now, I had no doubt.

When he turned slowly and faced me, I rested my hands on his chest. I leaned up and brought my mouth to his, pressing his lips until they opened. I whimpered when Cru finally let go of his restraint and our tongues met. He lifted me like he had earlier, and I wrapped my legs around his waist. He had to feel my heat in the same way I did his hardness. If our clothes weren't between us, he could slide his cock into me with ease; that's how wet I was.

He set me on the counter and spread my legs but pulled me toward him so my arse rested on the edge. With one hand, he held me in place while he snaked the other down the front of my jeans after releasing the buttons of the fly. He pushed my thong out of the way and touched my clit with the pad of his thumb, groaning when he realized I was bare.

"Please," I begged, breaking our kiss only as long as it took me to say the word.

He responded by inserting one finger into my pussy and increasing the pressure on my clit.

"Cru—" I cried, knowing if he didn't stop, I wouldn't be able to hold off my orgasm.

When he added a second finger, thrust, and pressed harder, then leaned down and nipped my breast with his teeth through my shirt, I shattered. I clung to him as the continued waves of pleasure left me dizzy and breathless.

He kissed me, transitioning from heated to gentle as I floated back to reality.

Cru leaned back, removed his hand from inside my pants, refastened the buttons of the fly, then kissed me again, trailing his lips from mine across my cheek to my neck.

I had trouble forming thoughts other than wishing we could cancel dinner. "When will they be here?"

"In a few minutes."

"Cru—" I repeated, but he stopped me from speaking with his lips, lifted me from the counter, and set me on my feet. As he walked away, I saw him bring his fingers to his nose and inhale. When his eyes closed and he touched the tips with his tongue, I came close to having another orgasm. He was so fucking sexy, so mesmerizing, so passionate that I couldn't wait until later, when our naked bodies writhed against each other.

I was already drenched, and just looking at Cru made my pussy weep more. "I need to put on different clothes."

"Wait." He returned to where I stood, gripping the counter.

"What are you doing?" I asked when he unfastened my pants again, pulled them over my arse, then knelt in front of me. He leaned forward, this time bringing his mouth between my legs.

"I need these." He wrapped the lace of my thong around his finger and pulled until it tore, then did the same thing on the other side. He removed them from my body, stuffed them in his pocket, then pulled my jeans back up and refastened them before standing and swatting my bottom. "Go change."

"I don't think I can walk." I wasn't exaggerating. I was too dizzy with renewed desire. I didn't dare release my grip on the counter.

"I can take care of that." Before I realized what was happening, Cru lifted me and slung me over his shoulder. One hand cupped my sex as he carried me upstairs, then deposited me on the bed.

"Don't go," I pleaded when he took a step away.

"We both know I have to." He rubbed his hardness. "As it is, I can't imagine how I'll make it through dinner without your parents and my mother and siblings knowing exactly how badly I want to fuck you."

My eyes rolled back in my head, and I flopped against the mattress, unable to stop myself from putting my hand between my legs.

I felt Cru's weight on the mattress but was still surprised when he wrapped his fingers around my wrist and pulled my hand away from my sex. "No touching yourself."

I opened my eyes and looked into his.

"You'll earn your pleasure tonight, Daphne."

"How?"

"Until our guests leave, you'll do as I ask."

"What do you mean?"

He kissed my cheek. "You'll see." He turned and looked out the window. "Better hurry. Your parents are here."

I groaned. "My parents?"

He nodded. "And it looks like they stopped to pick up my ma." He was on his way out the bedroom door when he stopped and looked over his shoulder. "Daphne?"

"Yes?"

"If you touch yourself again, I'll know."

I nearly convulsed, looking into his heated eyes. How could I be expected to focus on making dinner or conversation or anything other than how much my body yearned for Cru's?

"Wait," I said, racing after him before he went downstairs. When he turned toward me, I cupped his hardness, then ran a finger down his length. "If I'm going to suffer, so are you."

He pulled my body flush with his. "You have no idea how much I've suffered all these years. It started the day I met you, Daphne." He reached up and tweaked my nipple. "Do as you're told, and both our suffering will soon end."

I retreated to the bedroom when he went downstairs, carefully choosing what to wear. Cru had to know me well enough to expect I'd play the game just as well as he was.

When I joined him and our guests downstairs, I had on a short skirt similar to the one I'd worn before and a bra matching a different garter belt that held up another pair of the silk stockings I'd purchased. I wore a sweater and shoes but no panties—something I intended to make Cru very well aware of.

After greeting my parents and his mother, I stood in the kitchen, prepping the rest of dinner. Cru approached me from behind, shifted me so the lower halves of our bodies were obstructed from view by the island, and ran his hand up my leg. When he reached my pussy, his breath caught at the same time mine did.

I closed my eyes and leaned into him when he brushed my clit with his index finger. A split second later his touch was gone and he was headed to the door to greet Alex and Maddox. Even with broken ribs, I doubted Alex's husband was in any more discomfort than I was.

"Less getting up and down," he mumbled when he sat at a stool near the bar and Alex asked if he'd be more comfortable in a chair. "Good to see you, Daphne," he said, resting his elbow on the countertop and his chin in his hand.

I walked over and kissed his cheek. "How are you doing, Mad?" I asked.

"A lot better than I will be when the pain meds wear off."

"I've been where you are, so I can empathize."

"Yeah? How many did you break?" he asked.

"Four," I responded, returning to where I'd been air-frying nori.

He raised a brow. "Ouch. How?"

"Surfing." My cheeks heated when Cru stepped behind me for the second time.

"Anything I can do to help?" he asked as his hand trailed the same path it had earlier—up my leg until he reached the apex of my thighs.

"You can get your brother-in-law a drink," Maddox responded.

Cru squeezed me, then removed his hand. "What are you allowed to have?" he asked.

"Whatever the fuck I want."

When my eyes met Maddox's and he winked, I wondered if he'd picked up on what Cru had done. My cheeks flushed.

"Looks like Daph could use a drink too. Bring me a finger of bourbon. She might need two," he said, winking a second time.

I looked around the room. "Where's Trevino?"

"When they told me Maddox was being discharged, I messaged him, and he responded to head here without him. I expected him to have already arrived," Alex said when she approached and delivered our drinks. I thought she might give Maddox a hard time about adding alcohol on top of his medication, but all she did was kiss his cheek. "Can I help?" she asked.

I pushed the note I'd jotted in her direction. "If you'll find out what everyone wants, I'll start assembling tacos."

"What can I do?" my mother asked.

"The salad is chilling and only needs to be dressed."

"On it," she said, opening the refrigerator door and pulling it out. "This looks fantastic, Daphne," she said, removing the cling wrap and tossing it with the serving utensils I'd left on the counter.

I looked around the room until my gaze met Cru's. He held it, making sure I was aware when he reached into the pocket where he'd put the remnants of my panties earlier.

"Is everything okay, sweetheart?" my mum asked. "You look flushed."

I glanced down at the empty glass that had held the bourbon I'd finished in one drink. "I could use a glass of water."

She poured it and set it in front of me. "Anything else?"

"Yeah, I need to talk to Cru for a minute." I walked over to where he stood talking to his sister. "Have you heard from Bit?" I asked.

He shook his head. "This kind of thing isn't unusual from him. I just wonder where he went and how he got there, given I have his vehicle."

"I'm assuming you've tried reaching him."

Cru nodded. "It's going straight to voicemail."

"Should we wait?"

He looked at Alex, who shrugged. "No telling when he might show up," she said.

"It's fine, Daph. He'll eat when he gets here."

"I'd planned for us to sit on the terrace," I said, glancing over at Maddox.

"I can manage," he said, standing with Alex's support. She slid the list of what everyone wanted over to me before helping him through the doors that led out to the dining area.

Since everyone appeared to want one of each type of taco, my mother and Lucia helped me with the assembly, setting each inside the holders Cru and I had purchased at the home-goods store.

He, Alex, and my dad carried food out, then returned for more while my mum and Lucia went out to take their seats.

"Are you worried about your brother?" I asked when he came in ahead of the others.

He shook his head. "This is more like the Bit I know than the one who's been hanging around lately."

"This is the last of it," I said, motioning to the final platter when my dad returned.

"We'll be out in a minute," Cru said to my father.

Once he was out the door, leaving us alone, Cru leaned into me, pressing his hardness between the cheeks of my bottom. "Are you still wet for me,

Daphne?" he whispered, his warm breath teasing my ear.

I reached behind and between us. "Just as much as you're hard for me."

"This is going to be a very long night," he murmured.

"During or after dinner?"

"Both." He nuzzled my neck. "Do you remember I told you to do as I asked?"

"Yes."

"Good."

13

Cru

Earlier, I'd asked Alex to make sure two adjacent seats were open for Daphne and me. I took her trembling hand in mine and led her out to the enclosed terrace, pleased to see we'd be seated at the far end of the table, where no one would notice if I reached under it and put my hand between her legs.

I pulled the chair to my left out for her, avoiding the gaze of everyone else at the table. No doubt those here, including my mother, were watching and waiting for a sign confirming what I was sure they all suspected—that it had taken Daphne and me less than a few days to go from friends to lovers.

We weren't yet, but by sunrise, that would all change. I planned to take her to bed and make her mine in every way I could. By breakfast, I'd erase the memory of every man she'd been with before me. No one could love on Daphne's body the way I would, because no one loved her a fraction as much as I did.

Once seated, I rested my left hand on Daphne's thigh, then raised my wineglass with my right. "I'd like to offer a toast," I said at the same time she opened her legs, then used her left hand to guide mine between them. "To Daphne"—I turned my head to look into her eyes—"the newest member of the Avila and Los Caballeros family."

Glasses were raised, and the others at the table offered their congratulations, but I couldn't look away from her questioning eyes. When I nodded once, leaned forward, and brushed her lips with mine, I heard both gasps and murmurs of happiness from our families. After breaking our chaste kiss, I brought my mouth to her ear. "This is just the beginning for us, Daphne."

"I can't wait," she whispered.

I kissed her a second time. "Me either."

As I turned to face the table, the first person I saw was my ma. Her smile and the tears in her eyes told me everything I needed to know. She approved. Whether she did or not wouldn't have stopped me from pursuing a life with Daph; her happiness over it just made it sweeter.

"Do not make a sound," I whispered before digging into the food on my plate. I ate with one hand, refusing to take the other from between Daphne's legs. I alternated between cupping her bareness and stroking her clit. Thinking about putting my mouth where my fingers were almost had me groaning out loud.

All the while, she remained silent. The only time she spoke was in direct response to a question, and then, I increased the pressure on her sensitive bundle of nerves with every word she uttered. That she took my assault on her pleasure without pushing my hand away or asking me to stop made me hard as granite.

"Come on, Ma," said Alex when everyone appeared to be finished eating and she stood. "The least we can do after this feast is help clean up."

Daphne's mom stood too, and when she started to as well, I wouldn't let her.

"Stay where you are," I leaned in and said.

"Cru, I should help." Since it was the first she'd given me a hard time, I let it go. However, I couldn't assist either, something that appeared to give Daphne great pleasure, based on her smirk. Now, *that* would get her in trouble.

"Congratulations on bringing Daphne on board," said Maddox, raising what was left in his glass in my direction. I did the same and took a drink when he did.

"I can't wait to see what she makes," I said.

"Bringing Bradley on as winemaker at Butler Ranch was one of the smartest things I ever did. It took Naught a while to agree. I'd say he's pretty happy about it now, though."

Naughton had married the woman Maddox mentioned within a year of her taking over as head winemaker in his older brother's place.

Mad shook his head. "She makes damn good wine, just like I predict Daphne will."

"So what happened?" I asked. "How'd you break your ribs?"

He chuckled. "Don't ask."

"What did you do, slip and fall in the fermentation room?" The way his cheeks heated told me I wasn't far off. "Sorry, man," I said, chuckling.

He laughed too and looked between me and Daphne's dad. "I'd appreciate if you didn't let word get out."

"I don't know, fellas. Sounds like we should use this opportunity to get even with Maddox for all his high jinks over the years," said Noah. "What can we get out of him?"

"Withdraw the Demetria Cab from next year's awards," I muttered. It was the only category I hadn't been able to best him in, and each year, it pissed me off.

"What fun would that be?" he countered, still chuckling. "Winning by getting rid of your competition? No way would that make you happy, Cru."

"You're right," I said, knowing he was.

I saw lights from a vehicle approaching the house. "This must be Bit," I muttered. I watched the SUV pull in and park, but I didn't recognize it.

"What's up?" Maddox asked.

"It is him, but he isn't alone." When two men walked toward the house, I took a closer look. "I think Decker Ashford is with him. Would you excuse me?"

"Of course," said Maddox when I raced into the house.

By the time I was inside, they were both walking in the front door.

"Everything okay?" I asked, meeting them in the entryway.

"Is there somewhere we can talk?" Deck asked, looking behind me.

I glanced over my shoulder and saw everyone, including Maddox, had come inside.

"Sure, follow me," I said, leading them into the back bedroom. I stopped before going inside. "Should I get Daphne?"

"In a minute," Decker responded.

I shut the door behind us and looked between him and my brother.

"Go ahead," Bit said.

Decker cleared his throat. "After you and Daphne left the hospital, your brother went outside to take a break. He hadn't been out there long when he overheard two men talking. One said something about being able to grab 'her' once you returned to the ranch."

My eyes opened wide. "Do you think they meant Daph?" I asked.

"I know they did," Decker said, nodding. "Anyway, your brother was able to record the rest of their conversation, and it was pretty damning. When he heard them say it was time to head out, he went inside and called me. My team and I showed up right as they were exiting the parking lot. We surrounded them and waited for local law enforcement to get there."

"You were already here?" I asked.

"Affirmative. We'd been tracking three suspects we strongly believed were the ones who'd held Daphne captive back in New York. The problem was we didn't have enough proof to apprehend them."

"What about now?"

Deck put his hand on Trevino's shoulder. "Thanks to this guy, we have more than enough to hold them. The sheriff has them in custody, and I'm headed to the jail to interrogate them now. I figure one of them will be scared enough to confess and take the others down with him or her."

"Wow," I said, shaking my head and blinking away tears. I reached for Trev, and we embraced. "I don't know how to thank you, Bit."

"I was in the right place at the right time."

"And had the forethought to record their conversation," said Decker. "Without that, we might not have had enough to take them in. I've been building a case since you rescued Daphne, and I think we easily have them on kidnapping."

"I should tell her."

Decker nodded. "I need to head out, but your brother can answer any questions she might have."

"What about the others here?" I asked.

"All family, right?" he asked.

"Either mine or Daph's."

"I don't see a problem with you including them when you tell her."

Decker shook Trevino's hand. "You did good, Bit."

When he walked out, I followed. "I wanted to ask about your fee and who's taking care of it."

"Since it was a kidnapping and Daphne was essentially taken across state lines, the FBI has it covered."

"If there's anything extra—"

"There's not."

I watched the man walk away, then returned inside, looking for my brother. "You saved Daphne's life, Bit, and I'll be eternally grateful to you for it."

His cheeks flushed, but I also saw the flash of a smile.

"Come on. Let's go tell everyone the good news."

We weren't all the way through the story when Trevino's cell rang. He stepped aside to answer it but didn't leave the room. When he ended the call, his smile was broad.

"Decker said he's got a full confession. Apparently, when they first met her, the name sounded familiar, and they looked her up. Once they discovered she was the daughter of the owners of the Cullen House, they decided to cash in on their chance meeting."

I was already standing next to Daphne with my arm around her but gathered her closer. "You're safe now," I whispered.

"He's sure it's them?"

Bit's cell vibrated. "Are you up to seeing their mug shots?" he asked.

Daphne raised her head and looked into my eyes.

"It's up to you. It doesn't sound like you'll need to identify them. At least not tonight."

"I want to be sure," she said barely above a whisper.

I nodded, and Trevino approached. She took his cell and swiped between the images. "It's them," she said first to me, then to her parents.

While the three embraced, I walked over to Bit. "You did good, brother," I said, repeating Decker's earlier words to him.

"Trevino?" I heard our mother say from behind me. I stepped aside and watched as they hugged. I prayed she'd realize her earlier misstep and start treating Trevino like she did the rest of us.

"He's a hero," said Alex, walking up to stand next to me.

"He sure is." I put my arm around her shoulders and squeezed. After glancing behind us, I saw Daphne and her parents watching but no longer talking. "Excuse me," I said to my sister.

"I can't believe it's over," said Daph. "I don't even want to think about the fact they were here in Paso Robles."

"You're safe now," I said, pulling her close and kissing her temple.

"We don't know how to thank you," Noah said to me.

"Thank him." I motioned to where my brother sat on the sofa with our ma, Alex, and Maddox.

I thought Daphne would go with them, but she remained by my side.

"Thank you doesn't feel like enough," she said, watching her parents embrace Bit after he stood.

"I'm sure he'd appreciate leftovers."

"Right!" Daphne's smile was huge. "Help me?"

"Wanna hear how Maddox broke his ribs?" I asked when my sister's husband and Bit returned to the kitchen and sat on the stools by the island. Daphne's parents stood beside them.

"I do," my brother said before taking a big bite of one of the sushi tacos.

Maddox glared at me. "I never should've told you," he said under his breath.

"But now that you have, there's still the matter of what you'll give me in return for my silence." I turned to Bit. "I suggested he withdraw the Demetria Cab from competition this year."

"I have a better idea. Host the first wine dinner in the old tasting room with us," said Bit.

"What's this?" Maddox asked.

I let my brother take the lead, telling him about the work he'd done to restore the dilapidated building, and his suggestion that we host events in it, given its more intimate setting.

"I'm all in," said Mad when Trev stopped talking. "In fact, let's make a festival out of it."

Bit's face lit up. "When?"

"How's my husband holding up?" Alex asked when she and our mother joined us too.

"Fine. He and Bit are planning a festival here, at Los Cab. I think I heard them say it should take the place of the bachelor auction."

"Very funny."

I shrugged. "I guess you'll find out soon enough."

She glared at me. "You wouldn't dare."

"Try me."

"You're mean," said Daphne, leaning up to kiss my cheek.

"You have no idea how much shit I've endured from her when I was growing up. In fact, it continues to this day."

"Poor baby," she said, linking our arms and resting her head on my shoulder.

"Think we could skip dessert?" I asked at the same time I saw Beatrice take it out of the fridge.

"Not on your life," my mother said, leaning over to stick her finger in the whipped cream on top of the trifle.

"Ma!" I scolded.

"What? You did it enough as a boy. It's my turn."

"Can you pack some of that up to go?" asked Trevino, coming inside with Maddox and Alex.

"Pain meds are wearing off," my sister explained.

"Can I help?" I asked.

"Just don't touch me," said Maddox when I approached.

"I'll probably hang out at their house for a while," said Trevino after Alex led her husband outside.

I reached into my pocket and gave him his keys.

"Hang on," said Daphne, scooping trifle into a container. She put a lid on it and rushed it over to Trev, who leaned in and kissed her cheek.

"Thanks, sis."

"What do you say, Bea? Should we leave these youngsters on their own?" Daphne's father said to her mom.

"I have a very early start to my day. Would you mind dropping me off at the house?" my mother asked him.

"Not at all," he responded.

"Do you want some trifle to go?" Daphne offered.

"I'm too full," said her mother.

"Maybe just one more taste," said mine, sticking her finger in the whipped cream a second time. On her way out, she winked at me.

"Good night, Ma."

She leaned up and kissed my cheek. "Do the right thing, mijo," she whispered.

I intended to, eventually. Tonight, though, I had all kinds of wrong planned. Based on the look on Daphne's face, she was prepared for anything and everything I had in mind.

"Trifle?" she asked, dipping her finger deep into the cream.

I walked over and picked up the remote that closed the blinds on the main level of the house and turned off the lights everywhere but the kitchen.

She held up her finger as I approached. I grabbed her wrist and sucked it into my mouth. When I released it, I put my hands on her waist. "Pull your skirt up." After she had, I lifted her onto the kitchen island.

Daphne gasped when her naked bottom came in contact with the cold, hard granite.

"Now, this," I said, pulling her sweater over her head. "Lie back."

When she did, I pulled the cups of her bra out of my way, stuck my finger into the trifle like she had, smeared her nipples with the cream, then sucked one into my mouth, followed by the other. Her body writhed on the counter, and her back arched.

"Cru, please touch me."

This time, I stuck three fingers into the sugary dessert and coated the outside of her pussy with it. After lapping it away, I focused my attention on her clit. I knew she wanted my fingers, but first, I made her get them wet. "Suck," I said, inserting one at a time in her mouth.

Before putting them where she wanted, I used my lips and tongue, bringing her right to the brink of an orgasm, then pulled away.

Daphne weaved her fingers in my hair, trying to connect my face and her pussy, but I wouldn't budge. I needed the break to get myself under control. If I didn't, I'd explode the minute I was inside her.

I eased farther away, propped myself up with my arms on either side of her, and stared into her eyes. "I'm taking you into the bedroom, Daphne, where we're going to make love until the sun comes up. I'll make you come so many times you won't know your own name, and then I'll do it some more. Do you want to know why?"

"Why?" Her eyes bored into mine.

"I've spent the last eight years wanting you."

"Only eight?"

I smiled and lifted her into my arms. "That's as much as I'll admit to."

"It's only now that I realize I wanted you all along," she said when I rested her body on the bed. "I know that might be hard to believe, but it's true."

I stretched out beside her. "I know you wouldn't lie to me, Daphne."

She turned her head away. "I was so afraid you didn't want me."

"That makes no sense, Daph. You've known how I felt about you."

"Well, there was the thing with Anthony Ricci."

My eyes scrunched. "What thing?"

"Alex said he was happily involved with another winemaker at the same time you were talking to him."

I propped myself up on my elbow. "*Wait.* You thought I was gay?"

"No, well, I mean, maybe."

I shifted off the bed and practically tore my clothes from my body. "Do you have any doubt now that I'm not?" I asked when her eyes went straight to my erection.

"Um, no. None at all."

"Good." Any ideas I had about confessing the depth of my feelings for her or making slow, passionate love to her were gone. I went to the end of the bed, spread her legs, and positioned myself between them. "Dammit," I muttered, easing away.

"Wait," said Daph, grabbing my arm.

"I need a condom."

She reached inside the front of her garter belt and pulled one out. "Handy, right?"

I took it from her. "Do you have more?"

"The pocket is only big enough for one."

I looked at the logo on the foil before tearing it open. "Fanny Wrappers?"

Daphne nodded. "One with every purchase, and by that, I mean every pair of panties, stockings, thongs…"

"You must have a boxful."

"I do. Upstairs." She winked.

The smile left both our faces as I rolled it on, then moved between her legs, where I'd been a few moments ago. I dragged my cock through her wetness, pressing the tip against her clit.

Daphne reached behind me and grabbed the cheeks of my ass, pulling my body closer to hers. "I can't wait, Cru. The next time I come, I want it to be with you inside me."

My body responded out of instinct as I breached her entrance and thrust inside. Once wrapped in her lush flesh, I stilled, knowing I'd remember this moment for the rest of my life.

14

Daphne

Cru's eyes, riveted on mine, penetrated as much as his body did. Once he was as deep inside as he could be, he stilled, and my pussy clenched his cock as if by its own volition.

I'd loved Beau, or so I thought, but the connection between this man and me was much more powerful. I could *feel* his love, and it made my heart swell. I longed to say the three words that meant more than any other, but I couldn't bring myself to. I didn't want Cru to think it was only because I was swept up in the moment or that the way he made my body sing was the reason I was ready to finally admit the depth of my feelings for him—my love for him. It was so intense it nearly brought me to tears, and I closed my eyes.

"Daphne, don't shut me out," he said barely above a whisper.

"I'm not. It's the opposite. I'm so overwhelmed by what I feel…" Tears leaked when I gazed into the warmest eyes I'd ever known.

He brushed the hair from my forehead, cupped my cheek, then kissed me at the same time his body began to move again. He thrust slowly at first, then harder and deeper.

"Put your legs around me," he said, using one hand to lift my bottom. The change in angle caused him to swell and pulse. "Not yet," he said, even though his breathing accelerated and he only held still a few seconds.

"I'm going to fuck you hard, Daphne. We have all the time in the world to make love, but I need you in a different way first." He leaned down and sucked one hardened nipple into his mouth, then moved to the other. He adjusted me a second time, not thrusting again until I could feel him pressing against my G-spot.

"Fuck me, Cru," I begged.

Three words, very different than the ones I'd stopped myself from saying earlier, turned him into a man possessed. He pounded into me again and again, forcing my pussy to clench around him.

When I cried out, tightening my legs and arms, holding him as close to me as I could, I exploded with an orgasm so powerful it brought me to tears a second time. He brought his lips to mine in a passionate and possessive kiss, then I felt him convulse like I had. Did he know he'd just made me his? That I'd never be intimate with any other man again?

He shifted us to our sides without withdrawing from my body, draping my leg over his thigh.

"There are things I want to say—no, need to say—but I'm so afraid you're not ready to hear them," he said, stroking my lower lip with his finger.

I leaned forward and kissed his chest, right above his heart, then looked into his eyes. "I love you, Enzo. I have for so long. When I think about the time we wasted when we could've been together, the hurt is almost unbearable."

"You love me?"

"I do, and not as a friend. Although you are that. You're my best friend, my confidante, my hero, my protector, and now, you're also my lover."

He gripped my neck and brought his forehead to mine. "I feel like I've loved you all my life. I've longed for this. Yearned for it. No matter how often I told myself I shouldn't push you, I was too weak to give you the time and space you needed to accept the two of us as a couple."

I smiled. "I didn't need time, Cru. I only needed you. You're all I've ever wanted. I was just too stupid to see it."

"I love you, Daphne."

"I love you, Enzo."

He separated himself from my body and went to dispose of the condom. When he returned with another, I shook my head.

"I don't want anything between us."

"You're sure?" he asked.

"Completely. I have an IUD, so I won't get pregnant, and it's been a very long time since I've been intimate with anyone."

He knelt between my legs and positioned his already hard cock at my entrance but didn't breach my welcoming flesh. Instead, he rolled to his back, bringing me with him. I straddled him, and with his powerful hands, big enough to almost wrap around my waist, he guided me onto him, thrusting once so hard I almost had another orgasm.

"Fuck me, Daphne," he demanded, putting both hands on my breasts, capturing my nipples between his fingers, and pulling. In the same way he had, I let go, bringing us both to climaxes so brilliant I swore I saw stars.

Cru kept his promise of our making love until sunrise. As it came up on the horizon, he wrapped us both in the comforter he pulled from the bed and we snuggled on the porch swing, knowing that with the dawn came a new life for us both. We'd work together, our passion for making wine filling our hearts as much as our passion for each other.

Somehow, I knew I'd never leave the man who held me so close and made me feel safe and loved. I'd live out the rest of my days here with him, on the land his ancestors had made their home, and now, Cru and I would too.

My parents left to return to Australia two days after our dinner. When they'd arrived, I felt certain they'd try to convince me to go back with them. However, the subject never came up. We said a tearful goodbye at the airport after my father made Cru promise he'd take good care of me.

We stood side by side and watched them go through security, waving until they were out of sight.

"It seems more real now," I murmured.

"What's that?" Cru asked.

"My life here."

He brought my hand to his lips and kissed the back of it. "I hope it will be *our* life, Daph."

"Nothing would make me happier."

Our daily rhythm as the vineyards came alive was magical. As the heat of the sun intensified, so did our love for each other.

Throughout the rest of January and into the beginning of February, we continued to prune. With over six hundred hectares of vineyards, the equivalent of twelve hundred acres, planted with twenty different varietals, Cru and I had a lot of ground to cover. However, we didn't do it alone. What I'd never realized was the number of people Los Caballeros employed. During the slower times of year, there were still more than one hundred full-time workers. As the seasons progressed, it could swell to three hundred.

During the first few days, Cru and I visited every vineyard, double-checking those that had already been cut and making a plan of attack for those that still needed to be done.

With each we walked, Cru asked for my opinion before sharing his own. At first, it felt like a test. Soon, I realized he simply valued my input.

"The vineyards are immaculate," I commented on one of our daily walks.

"My father, then Brix, were insistent they be kept this way. It's no different than what they do in Spain. Californians are a little more lax."

I laughed. "Compared to Australians, they're not."

He chuckled too. It was a long-standing joke between us that it was anyone's guess whether a bottle of Chardonnay from Perth contained any of the varietal at all. The truth was our wine law was more stringent than that of the US; however, our growing, harvesting, fermenting, and bottling methodologies were where we could stand some code enforcement.

Since Los Cab's primary grapes—Cabernet Sauvignon, Merlot, Zinfandel, Syrah, and Chardonnay—accounted for fifty percent of what was planted, those were the areas we checked first. Next were Petite Sirah, Cabernet Franc, Grenache, Mourvèdre, and Petit Verdot, which made up another thirty percent. The remaining twenty percent was dedicated to experimental plantings.

As I learned, those were Cru's favorite and soon became mine too. I loved the way his eyes lit up when he showed me what he could grow that others insisted wouldn't thrive on the Central Coast.

Because my degrees were in viticulture, or grape growing, and enology, or wine-making, I found myself working with the vineyard manager on almost a daily basis rather than strictly with Cru.

"What would you like to do today?" Cru asked after we'd spent the morning lounging in bed rather than hurrying out to work. We'd promised each other we'd take a few days off since the month of February was slow and we'd done all the pruning we could without compromising the vines.

"Hmm," I murmured, gazing at the sunlight streaming in through the window.

"What day is it?" he asked.

Admittedly, I had no idea, and without looking at my mobile, I couldn't even guess.

I was relieved when he picked up his phone rather than forcing me to admit I was becoming just as bad as he was.

"It's the tenth of February."

"Is the date significant?" I asked.

"In a way. It means, if we wanted to, we could pay a visit to *El Lugar de Curación*."

"El what?"

"Tryst's ranch. It means the Healing Place. He built the house and other outbuildings for his wife Rosa. It's where they spent the last months of her life."

"How sad."

Cru shook his head. "It is, I suppose, until you're there. I don't know how to describe it, really."

"Addy said it's magical."

Cru thought about it for a minute, then nodded. "Spiritual too."

"I'd love to visit." I sat up in bed, not bothering to pull the sheet over my nakedness. If I had, Cru would only tug it away.

He typed something on his mobile, then set it down. Almost immediately, it pinged. "He says now would be the perfect time to come. I should also alert Brix."

While he did, I got up, went into the bathroom, and turned on the shower. I studied myself in the mirror while waiting for the water to warm up. I looked happy, and even though it was still winter in California, the freckles on my nose that came out when I spent time in the sun were visible. The most telling thing was the lack of dark circles under my eyes. I'd tried everything to get rid of them—creams, patches, cucumber masks—and nothing worked. Who knew that being with Cru could be the magic cure?

I'd just stepped under the warm water when he joined me. "What's on your mind, Daph?" he asked.

I giggled. "Truthfully, I was thinking about how good I look."

His gaze went from my eyes slowly down my body, then made its way up again. "Let me check the other side." When he spun me around and rested his hand on my arse, I giggled more.

"Yep, I'd say you look perfect. I should probably find out how you feel too." He spread my legs, put his hand between them, then ran his finger through my folds. "Better than perfect."

He turned me a second time. "What's going on, Daph?"

I reached up and put my hands on his shoulders. "I'm happy, Cru. Happier than I've been my entire life. I'm far less stressed, as evidenced by the lack of bags." I pointed to my eyes.

"It's all the phenomenal sex." His chest puffed out a little.

I leaned forward and ran my tongue around his nipple. "You're right, but there's more. I'm finally where I belong, Cru. I feel it deep in my soul. I've never known such contentment."

"It's all I've ever wanted."

I nodded. "Me too. It just took me a while to realize it."

15

Cru

After calling in a favor from another winemaker in the valley, I was able to arrange for Daphne and me to take a private flight to Álamos, where Tryst's ranch was located. I could've contacted Press or Beau, but I didn't want to. My relationship with Daphne was too new to involve either of them. It wasn't that I felt threatened or even that she'd be uncomfortable. It was more that I wanted what was between us to stay our business a little while longer. Her family and mine knew, and by this point, so did Roan Norman, or at least I hoped he did. Other than that, I wasn't ready to share our news.

"Tell me about it," Daphne said on the flight from San Luis Obispo to the airstrip Tryst had created on this ranch.

"I told you our house was designed and constructed using the traditional Indian architectural system known as *Vastu shastra.*"

She nodded. "I've been reading about it. It's quite fascinating."

"Tryst owned the property for several years before he built on it. The story is he was hiking in the area the day he first met the woman who would become his wife. He says the two were on a ridge, and he pointed to the valley below, telling her that's where they'd live once they were married."

"So romantic."

I wriggled my brows. "Runs in the family."

She smiled, leaned forward, and kissed me. "Tell me more."

"The first structure was a temple, followed by a water room. It's similar to a pump house, but like every other structure on the property, it incorporates Vastu principles."

"The science of keeping the five elements of nature—earth, water, fire, air, and space—in balance in order to maximize 'positive vibrational energy.'"

"You sound just like him when he talks about it."

"You miss him."

I leaned against the seat and sighed. "He's the only link I have to my father. The two were different as night and day, yet so alike. I can't explain it. Anyway, now, there's a main house, a meditation center, several casitas, and a therapeutic riding program."

"I can't wait to see it."

The plane landed an hour later, and out the window, I saw Tryst waiting with a golf cart. Brix was with him, and they both waved.

"It's tradition that the first place anyone visits on the ranch is the temple," I told her while we waited for the airstairs to be put in place so we could deboard.

"I'd love it."

"You know, I've been thinking about it and can't believe you and Tryst never met."

"We have, but it's been a while since I last saw him."

"Daphne, welcome," my uncle said, drawing her into an embrace as soon as our feet hit the ground.

"Hey, man," said Brix, doing the same with me. "Glad you brought her here."

"How's Addy?"

"Beautiful. Amazing. The reason the sun rises and sets each day."

I chuckled, but I knew exactly what he meant. I felt the same way about Daphne.

"I've arranged for you to stay in the sunrise casita," Tryst said when we hugged.

"I told Daphne we should visit the temple first."

"As well you should."

Our time on the ranch flew by. While we'd spent several days there, when it came time for us to leave, it seemed far too soon.

We'd made the most of our visit, riding out into the valley every day and talking and laughing over dinner with Brix, Addy, and Tryst. Daphne even tried to get me to do yoga with her every morning. After a couple of failed attempts, I told her I'd be happiest just watching her, which she thankfully agreed to.

Tryst was scheduled to meet us at the casitas to drive us to the airstrip, but when I saw him pull up, he looked troubled.

"What is it?" I asked, meeting him outside.

"I need to speak with Daphne." He brushed past me and walked in the front door. Rather than follow, I waited where I was.

"We're visiting the temple," she said when they joined me outside.

"Okay." I walked over to the golf cart.

"Not you," she said.

I looked between her and Tryst. "What's going on?" I asked.

"Trust, nephew," was his only response.

Daphne leaned up and kissed my cheek. "This seems important to him. He said we wouldn't be long."

I didn't like it, but I did trust Tryst enough to accept there was something he felt he had to discuss with Daph, and for some reason, they had to do it in the temple.

When they drove away, I went back inside and waited.

It wasn't long before they returned, maybe twenty minutes at the most. While Tryst seemed less anxious, Daphne's demeanor hadn't changed. She was as happy and relaxed as when we had breakfast together earlier.

"Everything okay?" I whispered when she greeted me.

"I think so."

"We should be on our way," said Tryst once I'd put our bags on the back of the cart.

When we pulled up to the plane waiting for us, I walked Daphne over to the airstairs. "I need to talk to my uncle. I'll just be a minute."

She kissed me and put her fingertips on my furrowed brow, rubbing it until I relaxed. "Go ahead. I'm fine, Cru. You needn't be so worried."

"What's going on?" I asked again when I returned to the golf cart where my uncle sat.

"It's for Daphne to figure out."

"What is?"

"When the time comes, I pray she clearly sees the right path."

I looked behind me, making sure she was inside the plane. When I saw she was, I sat beside him. "What's this about, Tryst? Are you thinking Daphne will want to be with Beau again? If you do, I can tell you that isn't possible. First of all, she doesn't want it. Second, he's with Sam now. They're engaged."

Tryst closed his eyes and shook his head. "Not Beau."

"You aren't going to tell me anything else, are you?"

His gaze met mine. "I am not, Enzo."

"What happened at the temple?" I asked Daphne an hour into our flight.

"Nothing, but everything, if that makes sense."

It didn't, but I nodded anyway. "What did Tryst talk to you about?"

"He didn't. In fact, he didn't go beyond the entrance."

My eyes scrunched.

She shrugged. "He told me to go in, stand in the very center under the skylights, and he'd wait."

"And then what?"

"As soon as I was inside, the sun broke through the clouds. I raised my face as the heat from it bathed me in light like I've never known. I turned in a circle, letting it wash over me. I cried, but I can't explain why. Then the light went away. I thought I'd feel cold, but I didn't. I only felt at peace."

Tryst's words, after all she'd just said, made even less sense to me. And, unlike her, the last thing I felt was a sense of peace.

16

Daphne

I had no idea what Cru and his uncle had discussed after I got on the plane when we left Álamos, and he didn't say. I also didn't understand the significance of Tryst taking me to the temple or what happened once I was inside. All I knew was with each passing day, I felt more and more like I belonged here—by Cru's side.

We'd been back in California close to a month when, on our morning walk amongst the vines, I saw the first sign of life by way of bud break. I raced over to check, and sure enough, I could clearly see green peeking through the gnarly, brown branches.

"Looks like it's time to get to work," Cru said as we inspected section after section and found the majority showing the same thing. Timing now started becoming crucial. Once the vines came out of dormancy, we'd have to eliminate suckers springing up near the base and anything else we found that might compromise hardiness.

As we cut and pruned, I noticed Cru following my lead, leaving everything on the ground, where it fell. Later, we'd return, shred, and till, turning the waste into what I believed was the most beneficial organic matter.

At night, we'd go to the house with barely enough energy to get out of our work clothes and eat. Yet once we'd showered and gotten in bed, it was as though, when our naked bodies touched, our stamina renewed, and we'd spent hours making love.

By May, flowering and fruit set were well underway, and by June, deep-green grapes were in abundance.

Every day was full of excitement and discovery, which would continue well into October, when the last of the ripened fruit was harvested.

I thanked Cru almost daily for giving me the opportunity to work at Los Cab and, thus, fulfilling a dream I almost didn't know I had.

"I love seeing you so happy," he'd say as often as I thanked him.

Cru had gradually convinced Trevino that he was *needed* in the vineyard, which was vastly different than offering him a job. While I was the second-label winemaker, he'd made Bit, as almost everyone called him now, vice chief of operations.

As I'd suspected all along, Bit knew a lot more about his family's vineyards than he'd ever let on. He'd also made great progress fixing up the original winery building. It was far too small to handle anything more than the experimental varietals, but that made it almost perfect. Rather than installing modern equipment, the original presses, and even the fermentation tanks, were rehabbed and made ready for the harvest that would begin in September and October.

Mid-July marked one of the most beautiful times in the vineyard—known as Veraison. It was a fancy word for berry ripening, when the color of the fruit transitioned from green to translucent, then golden, or in the case of the red varietals, turned shades varying from pink to purple.

Along with the change in color came the intense heat the valley was known for. Temperatures could reach well into the hundreds by ten in the morning.

"Ready for a break?" Cru said on one such day when he pulled up at the end of the row on an ATV. I'd been out less than two hours, but my shirt was already drenched with sweat.

"I'd love one."

"Hop on, then."

"Where are we going?" I asked when he sped past the house and up a hillside trail I hadn't been on before.

"It's a surprise," he said over his shoulder.

Once we entered the wooded area, the temperature dropped so significantly, and I groaned in appreciation. At the same time, I tightened my hold around his waist with one hand and reached between his legs with the other, relieved to find he was as aroused as I was.

"You're insatiable," he teased.

"Only with you, my love."

He turned his head far enough that, when I leaned forward, I could bring my lips to his. It was typically all it took to send my need for him skyrocketing.

Truthfully, just watching him walk toward me triggered the same desire I felt blazing in his eyes and made me want to jump into his arms, wrap my legs around him, and feel his hardness press against my pussy.

There'd been several days when getting in a cold, rather than warm, shower had been waylaid by our need to strip each other naked and make love, regardless of how sweaty we were.

When I saw the sun shining brighter ahead of us, I almost moaned in disappointment. However, when Cru pulled over and cut the ATV's engine, my eyes opened wide and I smiled in delight.

To our left was a pond fed by a waterfall that looked as though it sprung from the hillside. Beneath it was slate, which I knew without touching would be cold.

We jumped off the vehicle and stripped our clothes on our way into the water. I stuck my foot in its iciness at the same time Cru came up behind me, pressed his hardness into the cheeks of my arse, and snaked one hand down to my pussy.

"I've been waiting all month for there to be enough water to bring you here. Do you know how long I've imagined your legs wrapped around me as I held you in my arms, fucking you senseless as the stream cascaded over us?"

His words alone might've made me come, but the pressure of his fingers stroking me made it happen quicker.

"Cru!" I yelled out his name as he held my quivering body tight, not easing the assault of his fingers on my clit until I was convulsing. "God, what you do to me," I groaned, feeling my knees give out.

He lifted me in his arms and carried me the rest of the way. Once we were close, he lowered me so my feet were on the slate, then picked me up a second time, this time facing him. At the same moment I linked my ankles behind his back, Cru slid into me, then moved us under the cool current.

"Hold on tight, Daphne."

I shuddered, knowing precisely what was coming. Cru's powerful thighs made it easy for him to piston into me. He pressed my back against the moss-covered stone at my back, increasing his tempo and deepening his thrusts. I came at least twice before he pushed inside me one last time and pulsed his release.

We remained under the water, holding each other and kissing passionately. We'd made love every day since that first night, and each time felt better than the one before. Cru knew exactly how to coax my body into multiple orgasms with his hands, mouth, and cock, and I did the same for him. Two people couldn't possibly have been made more perfect for each other.

He eased himself from inside me, lowered me so my feet were on the slate, then took my hand and led me into the pond via the steps nature had carved out for us.

Once in the coolness of the spring-fed pond, he picked me up again when he realized how high the water level was. He could stand on the bottom and it reached his pecs. For me, I would've had to struggle to keep my head above the surface.

"I should call *you* Bit," he teased, kissing the tip of my nose. "But I have a better idea."

I trailed my tongue up the side of his neck. "What's that?"

He shuddered. "Don't distract me."

"Is this a distraction?" I asked, breathing warm air into his ear, followed by my tongue.

"If you don't stop, I won't be able to."

"Who says I want you to?"

He pretended as though he was about to drop me, and I squealed and clung to him. He gathered me back where I was and stared into my eyes.

"Daphne?"

"Yes, Enzo?"

"What would you think about me calling you Mrs. Avila?"

My gaze didn't waiver from his. "I would love it."

"You do know I'm asking you to marry me, right?"

"You'd better be since I'm already saying yes."

He turned while still holding me and walked toward the ATV. As he did, the pond grew shallower to the point where he could step out of it as if we were at the beach. He grabbed the shirt he'd draped on the handlebars and put it on the seat before resting me on it. Then he reached inside a storage box affixed to the back of the vehicle and pulled out two towels, along with dry clothes.

"If I didn't already love you more than I dreamed possible, it would increase exponentially right now."

He leaned forward and kissed me. "It grows deeper every day for me too."

After we both dressed, I thought we'd leave to return to the vineyards. Instead, Cru pulled out a cooler bag, spread the towels out on a grassy area, and we shared a picnic, complete with an unmarked bottle of wine.

"Is this what I think it is?" I asked, hoping it was the blend I'd first had at Stave.

"You'll have to taste it and find out."

I smiled and rubbed my hands together, watching as he poured into the two crystal glasses that had been inside the wine bag.

"It's even more intense than I remembered," I said after swirling and inhaling deeply.

"Go ahead," he said, waiting for me to taste first.

I savored the liquid that flowed over my tongue, experiencing every nuance and focusing on the mouth-feel, the dryness, as well as the acidity. I took a second sip, concentrating more on each flavor and when I experienced it. Its herbaceousness was more like red currant rather than true cherry but with a bold under-lying menthol note, followed quickly by boysenberry and blackberry compote. Finally, black licorice led into the long finish that had a tug of earth amid a generally velvety feel.

I looked up at him. "It's perfect."

While I watched him swirl, sniff, and taste, I thought about him saying that maybe someday he'd tell me what he'd named it.

"So?" I asked. "Do you agree?"

"I do. It's exactly what I wanted it to be."

"Does that mean you're ready to divulge the name?"

"Close." He winked.

I folded my arms and pretended to pout.

"There's one more thing I need to know first."

When he stood and held his hand out to me, I left the sandwich I was unwrapping on the towel.

"Look out," I warned when he took a knee almost directly on top of it.

The smile left my face as I watched him pull a small box from his pocket, then take my left hand in his right.

"Daphne Cullen, let's make this official. Will you marry me?"

"Of course I will. Yes, yes, yes!"

When I fell to my knees too and wrapped my arms around his neck, Cru hurriedly moved the sandwich aside, or I would've landed on it too.

He eased the ring on my finger, and I stared at it. "It's so beautiful."

"Do you like it?"

I shook my head. "I love it." There were five pear-shaped diamonds set on a platinum-colored band. The largest was in the center, and depending on the way the light hit it, it looked green or blue. The next largest flanked it, and the two on the outside were smaller but not by much.

"The first thing I thought when I saw the center stone was how much it reminded me of your eyes," he said, reaching into his pocket again. "This will be the wedding band."

The baguette stones in the second ring were the same color as the center diamond, and the two fit so perfectly it was hard to tell they were separate pieces.

As we sat on the towels near the pond, finally eating our picnic lunch, all I could think was how I'd never dreamed my life could be so perfect. I was engaged to a man I loved with all my heart and doing my dream job. So why wouldn't the dread I felt deep inside since the day we left Tryst's ranch go away?

17

Cru

I still hadn't told Daphne what I'd named the wine. Something inside me said the time wasn't right and to wait.

As much as I didn't want to, I knew we had to get back to the vineyards.

"We should go," said Daphne seconds after I'd had the same thought. "But we should celebrate tonight."

"Yeah? What are you thinking?"

She grinned. "I want it to be a surprise."

I took Daphne back to the section of vineyards where she and her crew had been working, then went to check on mine. When I returned a couple of hours later, she was standing near a vine, staring at her cell phone.

"What's wrong?" I said when I got closer to her and saw she was crying.

"It's my dad. He's had a stroke."

"Oh, God. I'm so sorry, Daph."

"That was my mum. She says I should come home."

"Of course. Let's go back to the house, and I'll book the flights."

She climbed on the back of the ATV after I had, and I raced out of the vineyard.

Once we were inside, I pulled out my laptop.

"We can catch a flight to LAX in two hours, then it's another two-hour wait to get on the one that will take us to Perth. I can try San Francisco and see if I can do better," I said, racing up the stairs to where she was packing.

"No, that's fine. I doubt there's anything quicker." She looked up at me. "Wait, did you say 'we'?"

"Yes. I'm going with you."

She dropped the clothes she was folding and stood in front of me. "You can't leave, Cru. There's too much to do. Especially with me gone."

"I don't care about that. The vines can wait."

She shook her head. "They can't, and you know it. Without Brix here, you're in charge."

"I'll get him to come back from Mexico."

She shook her head. "Let me get over there and see how bad it really is. Maybe I'll be able to return to the States in a few weeks' time."

A few weeks? God, I could hardly stand being away from her for a few hours.

She put her hands on my chest. "It'll be okay, Cru. Let me get home and see what Dad is facing in terms of his recovery, then I can make a plan."

The word home bothered me. This was her home. At least I thought it was. Or wanted it to be. I got it, though. She was worried about her dad in the same way I would've been.

I cupped her cheek. "I love you, Daphne."

"I know, and I love you too."

I waited until her plane took off from the San Luis Obispo airport before returning to Los Caballeros. Everything inside me screamed I should be with her, but she was right. There was too much work to be done in the vineyards for both of us to be gone.

At sundown, I called it a day and told the crews to go home and rest. Tomorrow would be another long, hot one. I was about to head to the house when my cell rang.

"Hey, Bit. What's up?"

"Where are you guys?"

"What do you mean?"

"You and Daphne. I've got everything ready."

I scrubbed my face. "Daphne's dad had a stroke. She's on her way to Australia."

"Wait. What? Shit. This isn't good. Damn, I wish I would've known."

"What do you mean you have everything ready?"

"Come by the old winery, and I'll show you."

I wanted to beg off, but it sounded like Bit needed me to meet him. "Be there in a few minutes."

I drove the ATV over and parked near where Daphne and I had tied off our horses. It seemed like a minute ago and weeks at the same time. I was already anxious to talk to her, and it would be hours before she landed.

When I walked up to the door, Bit was waiting just inside.

"She asked me to set this up. Said you were celebrating your engagement."

Strung lights crisscrossed the ceiling, casting a warm glow on the room. In the middle of the space, there was a table set for two. On it were candles, flowers, and an open bottle of wine.

The pain of missing her immediately felt worse.

"Sorry, man," said Bit.

"Thanks."

"Wanna eat?"

I didn't, but after all the work my brother put into this, I had to. It reminded me I'd wanted to ask him to screen in the sleeping porch that was off the second-floor bedroom. I wondered now if there'd be any reason to.

"You should've gone with her," he said thirty minutes into our dinner without us saying a word to each other.

"Too much to do in the vineyards," I muttered.

He shook his head. "Wine doesn't mean a thing if you aren't with the person you love. Nothing does."

As right as my brother was, I had too many people relying on me to just up and leave. July through October was our busiest time, and without me here to make decisions, a *helluva* lot could go wrong.

"What can I do to help?" he asked.

I rested my forearms on the table. "Help me find an interim winemaker to take over the second label."

"Done."

I looked up at him. "Who?"

"Me."

His air of confidence was enough to convince me to give him a shot. What else was I going to do if I didn't?

I was already up at six when my cell rang with a call from Daphne.

"How are you doing?" I asked.

"I just spoke with my mum. Dad isn't doing well."

"I'm so sorry, Daph."

Her breath caught. "I'm sorry too."

I waited, knowing she was crying.

"I miss you already," she said after a few seconds.

"I miss you too." Except it was so much worse than that. I felt as though part of my heart was already halfway around the world.

"I'll call again when I land," she said.

"Daphne?"

"Yes?"

"If you need me, I'll be on the next flight."

"I know you will. I love you, Cru."

"I love you, Daph."

It was another eight hours before I heard from her again. She was headed straight to the hospital and said she'd call once she knew more about her father. When I didn't hear after four more hours passed, I called her but had to leave a message when it went straight to voicemail.

"Hey, sorry to ring you so late," she said when I finally heard from her around midnight.

"Don't be. I'm up. How are things?"

"They rushed him into surgery shortly after I arrived to reduce the swelling in his brain. He's out now, and they're saying he's stable."

The more she talked, the more I felt as though I should be there with her. Maybe in the morning, I'd see if Brix would be willing to return from Mexico so I could fly to Australia.

I also needed to call my fellow *caballeros*, Beau especially since he was close to Daphne's parents, as well as Uncle Tryst. His generation referred to themselves as the Viejos, and while they'd all taken a step back when our generation took over, they still came to our aid when necessary. Now, it was one of their own who needed help.

I waited until after nine the next morning to call Beau, and as I'd anticipated, the news of Noah's stroke shook him.

"I'd ask why you aren't with her, but I know how tough things are in the vineyard this time of year. Any idea when she'll be back?"

"None."

"Let me know how I can help," he offered.

"You have a lot on your plate there too." Sam had inherited a large estate in a town outside Buffalo. It had vineyards and a winery, along with a cattle operation. She and Beau were in the midst of bringing the property back after years of neglect.

"We won't have much of a harvest this year. If necessary, I'll come out for that."

Harvest? That was at least two months away, if not three. Did he think Daphne would be gone that long? Or, like me, was he worried she'd never come back?

18

Daphne

"Mum, you should take a break, go home, and get some sleep."

"I can't leave him. What if he wakes up?"

My father had been in a medically induced coma for the two days following his surgery. I hadn't heard any of the doctors say they intended to bring him out of it.

"I'll check with the nurse."

I left the room, but instead of approaching the workstation, I walked over to the window. July was the coldest month of the year in Perth. Highs rarely climbed above eighteen degrees Celsius.

The vineyards here were in full dormancy, not that either my parents or I would be working in them if they weren't. Of the two hundred thousand hectares of grapes planted in Australia, my family owned more than half. Only a quarter of those were in Perth.

Two days ago, when my mother gave me an envelope containing my father's power of attorney, I discovered that, in the event of his incapacitation, I was expected to step in as interim CEO.

At first, I was furious he'd never discussed it with me. On the other hand, I was their only child. What had I thought would happen?

I desperately wanted to talk to Cru. More, I wanted to beg him to come be with me. I couldn't, though. Like me, he had responsibilities in California and people relying on him. While he wasn't an only child, there was no one else in their family who could take his place other than Brix, who was building a life in Mexico.

After the years Brix had sacrificed for the Avila family and for Los Caballeros, I knew Cru would never ask him to do more, and rightly so.

I checked the time. Two in the afternoon here meant it was nine at night in California. Deciding it wasn't too late to call, I rang Cru.

"Hi," I said when he picked up.

"Daph, it's so good to hear your voice."

His simple words, combined with my exhaustion, brought me to immediate tears. "I'm sorry," I said, wishing I could get a handle on my emotions.

"Don't be. I'm your person, Daph. You can cry with me just as much as you can laugh."

"I love you so much," I said, wiping the dampness on my face with the back of my hand.

"You sound tired."

"I'm so far beyond it. I'm practically delirious. My mum is worse, though. She's refusing to leave Dad's side."

"How is he?"

I explained about the coma and also that the doctors believed his prognosis was positive. At best, though, they predicted he'd have several months of rehab to complete after he was stabilized. At worst, he may have suffered irreversible brain damage.

The other thing I told him about was the power of attorney.

"Is there anyone on the board of directors you trust who can help you?" he asked.

"It's been so long since I've had anything to do with the business. I'm not sure I know many of them. I don't even know if Hewitt and Martin are still involved." Hewitt Ridge had been my father's best friend since they were in college together. Martin was Beau and Press' father and also a close friend of my dad's. Even if they were still on the board, they were based in the

States, so I doubted there was much they could do to help here.

"Have you spoken with either of them?" Cru asked.

"I haven't, but I should," I admitted.

"I can contact them on your behalf if you'd like?"

"Would you?"

"Of course, Daph. And just so you know, I alerted Beau and Tryst already."

I breathed a sigh of relief. After our exchange in Las Vegas, I dreaded calling Beau. I was sure he'd be sympathetic and kind, but truthfully, I was still miffed at him over the way he'd treated me, particularly after his mother passed. I'd been close to her for most of my life, and her death hit me hard. That Beau didn't have the decency to acknowledge how I might be feeling hurt more than I cared to admit.

I sighed, and tears flooded my eyes again. "I miss you so much."

"I miss you, Daphne, and I love you."

Our call ended with me promising to get in contact with him tomorrow unless there was news about my dad before that. We also agreed that our next call should be via video so we could see each other. The anticipation that we would gave me great comfort.

"Daphne?" I heard my mum call my name.

"I'm here," I said, walking toward her. "Is everything okay?"

"The doctors are on their way to speak with us."

I tucked my mobile away and followed her into my father's room.

Thankfully, they encouraged us to go home, saying my father was stable but they wouldn't consider bringing him out of the coma until tomorrow or the following day.

After getting my mum settled, I lay on the bed in what had been my childhood room and stared up at the ceiling. I prayed hard that when my father came to, his condition was better rather than worse. Regardless, I doubted I'd be able to return to California anytime soon.

I stared down at the engagement ring Cru had given me, pushing away thoughts that it would be impossible for us to consider marrying now. We'd figure it out, somehow, wouldn't we?

I covered my eyes with my arm and groaned. How, though? At least until my father came out of the coma, I'd have no idea how long I might have to remain in

Perth, and for the next three months, at least, it would be impossible for Cru to get away. I rolled to my side, pulled out my mobile, and studied the photo I'd taken without him realizing I had.

Everything about him was conveyed in the image. He was a beautiful man, with striking looks, a hard, muscular body, and a soul like none I'd ever known. Deep in my heart, I knew he loved me and always would, but would it be right to ask him to wait for me when it could be months, maybe even years, before I could return to Los Caballeros?

He'd certainly have to hire a second-label wine-maker right away. Maybe he already had.

I traced his face with my fingertip, wishing so much he was here with me now.

When my mobile rang with a call from him, I nearly fell off the bed.

"Could you feel me thinking about you?" I asked, staring into the face I already missed more than I dreamed possible.

"Hello, Daphne. As good as it was to hear your voice earlier, seeing you now is so much better."

"I was just looking at a photo of you," I confessed.

"Where are you?"

"Home, err, at my parents' house."

"What's behind you?"

"Hot-air balloons," I said, laughing. "I was obsessed with them as a child, so my mum had a mural painted of them." I moved so he could see it better.

"It looks like they're floating over a vineyard," he said.

"Good eye from thousands of miles away," I joked. "Speaking of the vines, how goes it at Los Cab?"

"Terrible."

I cocked my head but smiled. "Truly?"

"No. Everyone is stepping up, especially Bit."

"I'm so glad."

"He asked me to tell you that he's only keeping your place warm and to hurry home so he can get back to doing what he really loves."

"What's he doing now?"

"He's taken over your duties temporarily."

"Oh. Um. Wow."

"Daphne, you did hear me say it was temporary, didn't you?"

As ridiculous as it was, that I'd already been replaced felt like a knife to my heart. Yes, I'd heard it wasn't permanent, but what if it became that way? Every dream I'd had for my life came true only to be ripped away from me. I didn't blame my father or my mum. It wasn't their fault my dad had a health crisis. It also wasn't Cru's fault that he couldn't drop everything and come with me.

"Daphne?"

I looked at the screen, realizing every emotion I'd been feeling was likely playing out in my expressions. "I'm sorry. I just…" I wiped my tears.

"I love you so much," he said, putting his hand on the screen. I did the same, wishing so much I could feel his warmth through it. "I'm going to do everything I can to get there as soon as possible."

"It's too much to ask at this time of year."

"The alternative is for the crack in my heart to turn into a break, and soon, there will be nothing left of me."

"Cru…"

"That's how much I love you."

"I love you too." I hated that my words sounded flat in response to his beautiful confession of his feelings. "Talk tomorrow?"

"Of course. Sleep, my beauty. If you need me, I'm a call away."

When I woke the following morning, I immediately checked my phone for news of my dad. There were three missed calls from an Australian number I didn't recognize. When I called, the man who answered introduced himself as Steve Dorian, the chairman of the board at Cullen House.

His tone was cold, and that he hadn't first asked about my dad didn't sit well with me. "What can I do for you, Mr. Dorian?"

"The board has requested we meet with you as soon as possible."

"Regarding?" I asked.

"We have many matters to discuss."

"Would one of them be an inquiry about my father's health or perhaps how my mother is managing?"

He cleared his throat. "Of course."

"But as an afterthought."

"Ms. Cullen, you are in no position to—"

"I'll be in touch, Steve. In the meantime, do not contact me directly again."

"But—"

I ended the call and checked the time. It was four in the afternoon in California, so I rang Martin Barrett.

"Daphne, how is your father?" he said after picking up.

"We're not yet sure." I explained about the coma and my dad's current prognosis.

"If there's anything at all I can do, please reach out."

"I actually have a question for you unrelated to my dad. At least directly."

"What is it?"

"How well do you know Steve Dorian?"

"Slimy bastard," Martin muttered under his breath.

"He called a few minutes ago, saying he was the Cullen House's chairman of board. He requested a meeting with me."

"This isn't good," Martin muttered.

"Why? What's going on?"

"He requested my resignation as well as Hewitt's."

"When?"

"Yesterday."

"What the fuck, Martin?" I screeched, then lowered my voice. "Wait. I'm sorry. That was uncalled for."

"Don't apologize, Daphne. I've spoken to Hewitt, and we both believe he's attempting to take control of Cullen House."

"And force my father out when he's lying in a hospital bed in a coma?"

"I believe that is the case, yes. He's identified a vulnerability and intends to exploit it."

"My God, my father might *die*." I looked up and saw my mother standing right outside my door. "I've got to go, Martin."

"I'll be in touch, Daphne. Hewitt and I both have friends who are still on the board. I'll see if I can find out how much support Dorian has been able to finagle."

I dropped my mobile on the bed, took my mother's hand, and led her into the room.

"Who were you talking to?" she asked when we sat beside each other on the edge of the bed.

"Martin Barrett. Mum, how much do you know about Steve Dorian?"

"He's trying to steal your father's company."

"Does Dad know that?"

She nodded. "I think it's what led to his stroke."

"I'm sorry to ask this of you, but can you please tell me everything you know about it? About him?"

19

Cru

"When's the last time you spoke with Daphne?" Beau asked when I answered his call.

"A few hours ago. Why? Has something happened?"

"I got a call from my dad. He said one of the board members is trying to stage a coup."

"What are you talking about?"

"My dad thinks he intends to take control of Cullen House."

I walked from where I stood between rows of grapes over to the ATV. "Can he?"

"Apparently, he had enough votes to be named chairman. The next step would be to demand Noah be removed from both the board and the company. He's also called for my dad's and Hewitt's resignation."

"Daphne has Noah's power of attorney."

"My dad intends to fly over, as does Hewitt Ridge. They haven't withdrawn from the board yet. There are ten voting members currently, plus the chairman, who can only settle a tie. Hewitt, my dad, and Daphne make up three."

"So they need three more votes."

"That's right. They intend to see how it's looking. If it's promising, they'll call for a vote to oust the chairman."

"I'll go with them."

"Hold up, Cru. I don't think you should."

I clenched my fists. "Why not?"

"The biggest reason is the board might see your arrival as a weakness in Daphne. The second is so she learns she can do this without either of us intervening."

As hard as it was to admit, Beau was right on both counts. "I'll wait to hear what your dad and Hewitt find out."

"Listen, you understand that I don't mean to—"

"We're engaged."

"What did you say?"

"Daphne and me. I asked her to marry me."

"That's great!" Beau shouted. "Hey, Sam. Daphne and Cru are engaged." There was a pause. "She says congratulations."

"Thanks."

"When did this happen?" he asked.

"The same day her dad had the stroke."

Beau's mood shifted immediately. "God, I'm so sorry."

"Don't be. We'll figure this out one way or another. The most important part is I love her and she loves me."

"I hear you. I can't tell you how happy I am for you, Cru."

Beau ended the call, saying he'd be in touch as soon as he heard anything more about the situation with Cullen House's board.

I remained on the ATV and took several gulps of cold water. Today was the sixth day in a row with temperatures close to one hundred. On top of that, we'd had very little rain. When it did come, it was in a torrential downpour that started and stopped in under five minutes, nowhere near long enough for the moisture to penetrate the soil.

"Hey, Cru. Got a minute?" Bit asked, walking up to me.

"Sure. What's up?"

He opened his gloved hand and showed me the fruit and leaves on his palm.

"Fuck," I groaned when I leaned in and saw why he'd brought it to me. "Botrytis bunch rot."

He nodded.

The fungus was also known as noble rot. If caught during the flowering phase, we'd have the chance to eradicate it. As far along as we were with grape cluster, there was nothing we could do. "How bad is it?"

Bit pulled out a hand-drawn map of vineyard sections. There were marks on those where they'd found the fungus.

"Ten?" I asked.

My brother nodded. "Sorry, Cru."

"Don't be." The fungus was hard to catch and, once it took hold, spread at the same rate as a wildfire.

"Guess we'll up the off-dry production this year." I was being facetious, but about the only positive thing about Botrytis was that some of the most amazing sweet wines in the world could be made from the infected grapes.

"It's a rough year, Cru. Between this, the heat, and the drought, our numbers are going to be way down."

"I hear you, Bit."

Thankfully, the last few years had been really good and we had enough wine stored in barrels to keep this year's numbers up by releasing what we'd intended to be long-hold collections as well as increase our blend inventory.

"You're doing a good job, Cru."

I looked into my brother's eyes and saw nothing but sincerity.

"That means a lot, Bit. Thank you."

"There's something else I want to talk to you about."

I raised a brow. I'd heard enough bad news so far this afternoon and wasn't ready for more.

"I want to start hosting events in the old winery."

"Yeah? What's involved?" I asked.

"I should hire an event planner."

"You don't need my permission. This is your baby. Got anyone in mind?"

He shook his head. "I thought I'd run an ad."

"Excellent plan." I threw my leg over the ATV and started it up. "I'm calling it a day. Let everyone know they can take off, would you?"

"You got it, boss."

I was about to drive away when I put on the brakes. "Hey, Bit?"

"Yeah?"

"I love you, man."

"I love you too, Cru."

Rather than lie on the bed in the downstairs room, I climbed the stairs to the one Daphne and I had shared most often. I opened the dresser drawers, relieved to find she'd left most of the lingerie we'd purchased together here. The closet was over half full too.

Stretching out where she and I had last made love and rolled over, I inhaled her scent on the pillow, missing her so much I ached. While I understood Beau's reasons for suggesting I hold off traveling to Australia, it was damned hard to do. I wanted to stare into her eyes, touch her skin, and make love all night like we did before she left. Mostly, I just wanted her to come home so we could pick up where we'd left off.

For months, we'd both had everything we wanted in life. Most importantly, each other, but working together had been a dream come true too. I prayed she'd return before harvest and that she and I could still make wine together this year, even with the low yield, it looked like we'd experience.

Rather than sitting around, feeling sorry for myself, I got up, took a shower, and drove to Demetria, the vineyard property Maddox and Alex owned.

Up for company? I'd sent a text asking.

Sure. Maddox and I both need a change of scenery. How soon can you be here?

On my way now.

Speed.

I pulled through the main gate when Alex sent the signal to open it, then drove up the winding road to the top of a hill, where their villa and winery sat.

Los Caballeros was one of the most beautiful ranches on earth, in my opinion, but even I had to admit Demetria was something special.

Alex and Maddox were outside, on the terrace, when I walked up after parking.

"What's shakin', bro?" said Alex when I sat at one of the bistro tables and poured myself the last glass of wine from an open bottle in front of me.

"Nothing much good."

When she asked me to elaborate, I told her about Daphne's father's stroke and that Beau had said his father thought one of the Cullen House board members was attempting a hostile takeover.

"If that isn't bad enough, Bit discovered a spread of Botrytis bunch rot."

"We've got it too," said Maddox. "Fucking climate change. Naught's workin' on it if you want me to send him your way."

"I'd appreciate it." Naughton was Maddox's younger brother and something of a phenom in the wine industry. He was a viticulturist who was often referred to as the vine whisperer.

"I have a feeling there's more," said my sister, studying me.

When Alex's eyes bored into mine, I knew I didn't stand a chance. She had a way of needling people enough that they'd eventually cave and tell her everything she wanted to know.

"I proposed, and Daphne said yes."

Alex jumped up, raced over, and hugged me from behind. "Congratulations!" She held up the empty bottle. "I think we need another."

Maddox looked beyond me. "Hey, here's Naughton now."

As the two middle children of big families, Naught and I had always gotten along well.

"Los Cab has a Botrytis outbreak," Maddox told him.

He shook his head. "Whole fuckin' valley."

"And the west side," Maddox added.

"Not as bad, though. When did you find it?" he asked me.

"Bit did a few hours ago."

He nodded. "What are you doin' now?"

"He's having another glass of wine," said Alex, coming out with something sparkling.

Naughton stood and nudged me. "Come on. Let's go save your harvest."

"Hey, what about mine?" hollered Maddox.

"Los Cab's fungus will spread to my vineyards. Yours won't."

I followed him to where I'd parked. "Meet you there?"

"Yeah. I gotta stop and pick up some shit, then I'll be over. Did you let your crew go for the day?"

I nodded.

"Get 'em all back."

He took off down the driveway, throwing rocks in his wake while I called my brother and told him what was happening.

"I'll start making calls," he said. "Oh, and before you hang up, what do you know about Eberly Warrick?"

"Warwick?"

"Yeah. That's it."

"Not much. She's quite a bit younger than us. Her dad was in Los Caballeros with Pop, though. Why?"

"She applied for the event-planner job."

"That was quick."

"Right. Okay, I gotta go and rustle up the crews," he said, ending the call before I could say anything else.

A few years ago, Los Cab—the winery—had gone organic. I hoped that whatever Naughton's magical cure for the fungus was, it wouldn't jeopardize that certification. On the other hand, if we didn't have grapes to harvest, what was the point of being organic?

20

Daphne

By the time my mum finished telling me what she knew about Steve Dorian, I was as baffled as I was angry.

Another Cullen House board member had recommended the man to fill a vacant seat, and within six months, some of the members who'd been with my father for years had resigned. Not long after, Dorian had called for my father to step down as chairman. Either that or relinquish his role as CEO.

"Why did Dad go along with it?" I asked.

"He was made to believe it was for the good of the company. That is the role of a board, Daphne. Your father always listened to recommendations, based on his belief they all shared the same goals."

"It didn't occur to him something was up when his formerly trusted advisors started resigning?"

"In hindsight, maybe it should've, but it didn't. We can't go back and change it, Daphne," she snapped.

"Sorry, Mum. I'm just trying to understand."

"Before his stroke, I believe he may have uncovered something about Dorian that would've given him reason to have him removed from the board."

"What?"

She sighed. "If I knew, I would say so."

"Sorry," I repeated, this time under my breath.

Admittedly, I'd wondered why everyone went along with this guy. Was he paying them off? Or was there something more to it?

"I need to get to the bottom of this."

"What do you have in mind?" my mum asked.

"Mrs. Stanhope."

My mother's eyes lit up for the first time since I arrived in Perth. "Good thinking."

The woman had been my father's long-term secretary and would know more about the former and current board members than anyone other than him.

"Oh, Daphne, I'm so happy you're home. It will mean the world to your father," she said when she answered my call.

"I'm sure you've been very worried about him."

"Your sweet mum has given me updates, but you're right to say I worry."

"We, meaning my mother and I, were wondering if you'd like to meet us for lunch tomorrow. Maybe somewhere near the hospital? That way, we can tell you more about what's happening in person."

"Oh, I'd love that, dear."

"Also, would you mind bringing a list of the current board members with you? I'd like to contact each one personally."

"You're so much like your dad. He would want to do the same thing."

"Thank you so much."

"It's my pleasure, dear. I'll also bring the dossiers I was preparing for Mr. Cullen about the current board members." She cleared her throat. "That Dorian fellow, in particular."

"You're a wonder, Mrs. Stanhope. Thank you again."

"I'd have to be to keep up with your father, Daphne. Mr. Dorian and some of the other men on the board thought they could pull one over on him, but they were wrong."

"See you tomorrow, then," I said after she suggested a place to meet.

My mum was still standing in the doorway when I rang off.

"Mrs. Stanhope is right about one thing. Actually, more than one. First, you're just like him, and second, he would be very proud of you."

"I guess you overheard."

"Of course I did, sweetheart. The woman is eighty if she's a day and speaks at the same volume she wishes others would so she can hear them. The other thing she was right about was that, while Dorian thought he was getting away with something, your father *would* have stopped him."

"It's now my gauntlet to carry, and I won't let you down. You and Dad have worked too long and too hard to build Cullen House to let someone steal it out from under you."

She came over and sat next to me on the bed. "Daphne, I appreciate how much you're taking on, and even though your father can't say it yet, he will too."

"What else would I do? I'm your daughter."

She hugged me. "Some might not be so willing to set aside their own lives—their hopes and dreams—to help their family."

I nodded. That's exactly what I was doing. Setting my own life aside. Not just that, but I was turning my back on love too. But wouldn't they have done the same for me? Hadn't they given up a lot to raise me and make sure I was able to attend university? Live halfway around the world?

And what of Cru? He was doing the same thing in essence. He was the only one of the Avila siblings willing to take on their family's winery. More, their heritage. I was happy to hear Bit was helping, but how long would that last? Cru would never be able to do what Brix did. He'd never be able to tell his brothers and sister that he was moving out of California and someone else would need to run the family business. Not only couldn't he, but he wouldn't want to. Los Caballeros was his life.

The more I realized what was at stake here in Perth, the more I accepted that the fate of Cullen House lay solely in my hands. It was my heritage, and I had to be the one to save it.

When we arrived at the hospital a few hours later, my father's doctors were waiting for us.

"We believe he's ready to be gradually taken out of the coma," the lead physician told us.

"What's involved?" I asked.

He explained sedatives were keeping my father in a state of unconsciousness and, when the dosages were lessened, he'd become more and more alert. "The first thing that will happen is he'll open his eyes. From there, we'll see how he responds to speech."

I'd brought both my laptop and a book with me to the hospital but found I couldn't concentrate on anything other than waiting for my dad to come to. My mum was the same way.

Thinking about him opening his eyes and the first thing he saw being the two of us staring at him, made me laugh. Once I started, I couldn't stop. At first, my mum glared at me, but when I explained why I was chuckling, she got the giggles too. So instead of two people staring at him, my dad opened his eyes to his wife and daughter laughing uncontrollably.

"*Noah!*" My mother gasped. She stood and stroked his brow. "I love you so much," she said before bending down to brush his lips with hers. My dad blinked a few times but didn't say anything.

I stood on his opposite side and, like my mum, told him how much I loved him, then kissed his cheek.

"Daphne," my mother whispered. "Let the nurses know he's awake."

"I'll be right back, Dad," I said, kissing his cheek a second time.

I rushed from the room, and before I reached the desk, my mobile rang with a call from Cru.

"My dad is awake!" I exclaimed. "Just now. I need to tell the nurses."

"Daphne, I'm so happy to hear this news! Call me when you can."

"Sorry."

"Don't be. Do what you need to do. I'll be here."

"Thanks, Cru. I love you." I cringed when I hit the button to end the call before he could say it back, but I knew he'd understand.

My mum and I were asked to leave my father's room periodically throughout the rest of the day and evening, but we refused to go home. If there was a chance he'd speak, neither of us could stand the idea of missing it.

Instead of meeting Mrs. Stanhope somewhere outside the hospital, she agreed to come to the cafeteria when we told her why we didn't want to leave.

After we chatted for a few minutes and ate a light lunch, my mum excused herself. That was when my dad's secretary pulled out an expandable document holder that appeared full.

"If there's anything else you need, dear, just let me know and I'll keep digging."

"My mother said that, before his stroke, she believed he may have uncovered something about Steve Dorian that would've given him reason to remove him as chairman."

"I'm sorry, Daphne. If he did, he didn't say anything to me."

I patted the envelope and thanked her. "As soon as my dad is ready for visitors, I'll put your name first on the list."

Later in the evening, my mum and I decided to return to the house to rest. As we were leaving my father's room, we were met by his neurological team. Based on various tests they'd run, they determined my father had lost his ability to speak and walk, but functionality in his hands and arms seemed strong. They assured us, though, that he could recover fully. It would just take work.

I glanced over at my dad and saw he was trying to say something. I leaned in closer. "What is it?"

The only sound he could make was that of a W. However, I knew what he meant. He was willing to do whatever was necessary, put in all the work he had to, in order to recover.

In the weeks that followed, while my father struggled with rehab, Martin and Hewitt—who'd arrived a few days ago—and I were equally challenged by the Cullen House board of directors.

We'd met with each individually, at first, under the guise of introducing me as the interim member carrying my father's proxy.

Unfortunately, after several days of trying to change the minds of some of the men who knew my father well, it was still five against five—which meant Steve Dorian would cast the last vote to break the tie and demand my father's resignation. It didn't seem to matter that my dad was incapable of tendering it.

The man was also pushing for Martin and Hewitt to resign. Instead, they remained steadfast in their determination to help me regain control of the business my father and mother had built from the ground up.

I was about to get in the car to leave for the rehab center to see my dad when Martin met me in the driveway near where he and Hewitt had been staying in two of my parents' estate's guesthouses.

"Daph, I'm glad I caught you. We need to return to the States this morning for an emergency meeting later in the week. We'll return as soon as we're able. I apologize for this."

"I understand. I've already taken too much of your time as it is. I fear it's a lost cause." It broke my heart to admit it, but no amount of begging, pleading, or cajoling had resulted in any of the remaining members being willing to change their vote. "At least let me give you a lift to the airport."

"We'll take you up on it," he said when Hewitt joined us. "If we don't, we might miss our flight."

21

Cru

Daphne and I spoke almost every day, but with each that passed, I felt us growing farther apart. While we didn't acknowledge it in our phone calls, it would be six weeks tomorrow since she left California. No doubt she knew the passage of time, given it was equal to when her father had his stroke.

From what she said, he was recovering, just at a pace that frustrated him more than Daphne or her mom. Consequently, Noah was surly and unpleasant to be around, not unlike myself.

Most of the time, I barked orders rather than ask, to the point where Bit had suggested we have a meeting first thing every morning so I could outline my expectations and he could make sure most of them were accomplished.

It seemed as though every time I glanced in a mirror, I looked more like my dad. The stress of managing all the vineyards on my own and the amount of time I spent in the sun made me look haggard. Worse was the perpetual frown I wore. It was the same expression I'd seen on his face in every candid photo taken of my dad in the vineyard. I remembered seeing them when I was a kid, wondering why he'd done a job that required he work seven days a week and left him so miserable. Now, I understood.

"How's Daphne?" Bit asked when he walked into my house like he did every morning.

"Call her yourself and ask," I snapped since she and I hadn't been able to connect yesterday or the day before.

"Sit down."

I was dumping my coffee in the sink but spun around to see if it was me he'd just talked to like I was his pet dog.

"What the fuck, Bit—"

"I said to sit down."

I grabbed the barstool hard enough it almost toppled over, but I righted it and took a seat. "What's up?"

"You need to go see Daphne."

I smirked. "Right. And who will take care of things when I'm gone?"

He got closer to me and leaned in. "I will, mother-fucker, just like I have been."

"Are you saying I'm not pulling my weight?"

He scoffed. "You work your ass off every day, but no one wants to come within ten feet of you."

"Smell that bad, huh?"

"No, you're that much of a dick."

"You seem to have forgotten your place, little brother. I'm the boss. Not you."

He shook his head. "You remind me so much of Brix right now. How he was before he got together with Addy. He was just as miserable as you are now."

"Throw all the insults my way that you want. Nothing hurts, Bit. I'm numb."

"That isn't it, Cru. You're in so much pain that you can't feel anything else."

I hung my head, wishing I hadn't dumped my coffee since I didn't feel like getting up and making another cup even though I could sure use one.

"Daphne doesn't have time for me to visit. She's got her hands full, helping Noah recover and trying to save Cullen House."

He pulled out another stool and sat beside me. "Maybe you should consider helping *her*."

My mouth hung open. "It's the middle of September. We have to pay attention every single fucking day to what little we still have hanging on the vines and decide when to pick. Do you even know how long it takes to get to Australia? Sixteen fucking hours. That means thirty-two hours of travel time just there and back. So, what? I see her for an hour, turn around, and come home? Is that what you're suggesting?"

He folded his arms on the counter and shook his head. "You know we won't be picking for a week at least. If you don't think I can handle it, ask Naughton Butler to come over and check for you."

I'd never known my brother to stand up to anyone the way he was to me now, even before he was attacked in the caves. As angry as I was, I had to respect what he was trying to do. However misguided it actually was.

"Look, I appreciate this, but I *cannot* leave. When the harvest is finished, then I'll go."

"Okay. You've left me no choice." He stood. "I'm here on behalf of the Los Caballeros' workforce. Either you leave for Australia on the first flight out tomorrow, or we walk."

I thought my eyes would bug out of my head. "You walk? What the fuck does that mean?"

"It means there will be picket lines at every entrance to Los Caballeros. Work will not commence until we have a signed contract stating you're leaving the country and are on your way to Australia."

I got up, but rather than get another cup of coffee, I grabbed a bottle of bourbon from the pantry. I poured two fingers, finished them in one shot, then poured two more. "This isn't funny, Bit."

He stood his ground. "It isn't meant to be."

"I *can't* leave."

"Wrong, Cru. You can't *stay*." He looked at his phone. "I'll be back in one hour. You can give me your decision then."

Whether it was because of the liquor or just that my brother had worn me down, I started to laugh. Once I had, I couldn't stop. When I finally did, I stared at him with scrunched eyes. "Thank you, Bit."

"One hour, Cru."

I shook my head and glanced down at my phone. "My flight from SLO to LAX leaves in ninety minutes. I need you back here in far less than an hour."

"I have a better idea. I'll just stay here until you're ready to leave."

"I should probably check with Daphne first."

"No. Just go."

I got out of Bit's SUV when he pulled up to the departure area and got my bag out of the rear seat. The front passenger window was open, but when I went to say goodbye and thank him, I saw he was on the phone.

"That's right. The Los Cab caves at nine on Wednesday. Everyone will be there," I heard him say in a hushed tone of voice.

"See ya, Cru," he said, setting his phone on the console. "Gotta get back to work." He put the SUV in gear and sped off before I could ask what was going on.

Instead, once I was inside the terminal, I sent a message to Beau.

Do you know anything about a meeting at Los Cab two nights from now?

I didn't receive a response from him before the plane took off, after we landed in LA, or when we touched down in Sydney. The only time Beau had ever taken that long to answer a text from me was after his mother passed away and he'd disappeared.

I sensed something was going on; however, since I was already halfway around the world, did it matter?

22

Daphne

I was about to pull away after dropping Martin and Hewitt at the airport terminal when someone caught my eye. I turned off the car and jumped out.

"Cru?" I yelled, waving my hands and rushing in his direction.

"Daphne?" he hollered back.

"Miss, you can't leave your car there. This is a loading zone only," said a traffic monitor, blocking my way.

"It's okay. I'm loading. Or I'm about to." I stood on my tiptoes to look over his shoulder and saw Cru within a few paces of us. "That's my boyfriend, err, fiancé." I pointed behind him.

"That's right. I'm her fiancé," said Cru, pushing past him and lifting me in his arms.

I had no idea whether the traffic guy stayed or left. All I could think about was the kiss Cru and I shared, about the way his arms felt around me, and my elation that he was here. I didn't care why. Just that he was.

He set me on my feet, and we rushed over to my car, where the traffic guy was in the process of writing me a ticket. I sped off before he could finish, and in the rearview mirror, I saw him rip it up.

"I'd ask why you're here when you're supposed to be tending the vineyards, but I don't care. I'm just so happy to see you." I reached over and squeezed his hand.

"It's Bit's doing. Either I left or the workers would strike."

My eyes opened wide. "Seriously?"

"I'm not sure, but he was convincing enough for me to listen." He looked out the passenger window. "I've never been to Australia."

"Sadly, this is the worst time of the year to visit, much like California in the winter."

I glanced at him, and he was studying me. "Everything looks bright and beautiful to me. So, where are we headed?"

"My plan was to visit my father this morning, but I'll take you to the house instead."

Cru shook his head. "Let's see him first, unless you think he won't want me there."

"Not at all. He adores you. Plus, it gives him the chance to speak to someone other than my mum, the rehab staff, or me. I'll warn you, though, his words come quite slowly. He struggles, and at times, it can take several minutes for him to complete a sentence. The staff asks we not try to fill in the blanks for him."

"Understood. So, how do you feel about the progress he's made?"

I sighed. "It's one of those things that can be seen both positively and negatively. On one hand, he *is* making progress. On the other, he gets frustrated by how long it's taking. Honestly, my mum and I do too."

"Have you made any headway with the Cullen House board?"

I shook my head. "We're still tied in terms of how the members have said they'd vote, which means the chairman settles the tie. The reason I was at the airport was because Martin Barrett and Hewitt Ridge, who still sit on the board, were called to return to the States."

"Do you know why?" Cru asked.

"Martin said something about an emergency meeting." I glanced over when he didn't respond. His brow was furrowed. "Are you aware of what it's about?"

"No, but after Bit dropped me at the SLO terminal, I overheard him on the phone saying everyone would be at the Los Cab wine caves tomorrow night at nine. He left before I could ask what was going on, and my messages to Beau, asking if he knew, have gone unanswered."

"Why would he schedule a meeting in the caves of all places?" I asked. "Actually, never mind, I'm sure it's quite hot on your side of the world."

"That's not why."

I pulled into the rehab car park. "Why, then?"

He removed his seat belt and turned to face me. "I'll tell you, but not yet. Let's wait until after we see your father."

"Very mysterious," I said, smiling. "But, sure, if that's what you'd prefer."

As I'd anticipated, my father was thrilled to see Cru. His smile, which had been droopy from the time he came out of the coma, was getting better. Unless someone knew he'd struggled with it, they wouldn't guess he'd had any facial paralysis at all.

He was seated in a chair, eating lunch, and since his hand-eye coordination was the least compromised, he gave the appearance of being perfectly fine. It was only his inability to speak clearly, or walk, that gave away his actual condition.

"Hi, Dad," I said, leaning down to kiss his cheek while my mum embraced Cru.

"I didn't know you were visiting," I heard her say.

"It was a last-minute trip."

"Daphne didn't mention it."

"I didn't know. In fact, it was by chance that I was at the airport, dropping Martin and Hewitt off, at the same time Cru exited the terminal."

"Fate." All three of us turned when my father spoke.

"Yes, Dad, it certainly was."

"Belong...together."

My eyes filled with tears, making me wish I'd told my parents Cru and I were engaged. It didn't seem right to do so, given it would only cause them to question whether I should remain in Australia when the reality was I had no other choice.

My mum was aware of the issues with the board, but we hadn't informed my dad, and he hadn't asked.

There was the chance he didn't recall what he'd learned right before the stroke.

Cru glanced at my bare left hand, and his eyes scrunched, most likely realizing I hadn't let on that he'd proposed and I'd accepted.

We stayed another hour, then when my mum suggested Cru had had a long flight and might want to rest, we took it as an opportunity to leave and be alone, which we both desperately needed.

"I haven't told them yet," I said once we were in the car, but I hadn't started the engine.

"You don't have to explain, Daph." He reached over and took my hand.

"I just felt like it might cause them more stress."

Gazing into his eyes, I was reminded that Cru had always been patient with me, always understanding, always accepting. No matter what I'd done or what might have happened, he was forever my stalwart supporter. "I don't deserve you," I murmured like I had more than once in the time I'd known him.

Cru shook his head. "That's because your previous boyfriends never treated you right."

I chuckled that he'd used the plural form of the word when we both knew there was only one man he was referring to.

I started the car and was exiting the parking area when I realized that, if we went to my parents' house and stayed in the room I'd had as a child, we'd be forced to sleep in a bed hardly large enough for me, and definitely not for the two of us. I pulled over and rang the housekeeper, asking if she would please get one of the guesthouses ready for us. I was relieved when she said both accommodations Martin and Hewitt had vacated this morning were clean and available for the next guests.

"I hope you'll at least let me see the balloon mural," Cru teased when I ended the call.

"It's embarrassing, really."

He stroked the back of my hand with his thumb. "Everything about you is fascinating to me, Daph."

I shook my head, and my eyes filled with tears. "You're so good to me, Cru."

He smiled. "It's because I love you."

While I'd feared it might be awkward between us, the minute we walked through the front door of the guesthouse, we tore at each other's clothes. Our mouths were fused when we tumbled into the bedroom and fell on the mattress, already naked.

"I need you, Daphne," Cru said, positioning his hardness at the entrance to my drenched pussy.

"I need you too, Cru."

Unlike the languid lovemaking he and I had had in the past, this was fast and hard, our passion for each other equally frenzied. Our bodies were intertwined in every way they could be, as if we couldn't bear it if there was a place where our skin didn't touch.

Our orgasms came quickly and simultaneously. Still, we held each other tightly, both overwhelmed by the emotion of being together again.

I loved Cru with all my heart, but that didn't mean I knew what would come next for us. The best-case scenario was, once harvest ended in California, the grapes had been processed, and fermentation began, *maybe* he'd be able to return to Australia.

My parents might be able to manage for a few days or weeks without me in terms of my father's rehabilitation, but until matters were resolved with the board of Cullen House, I wouldn't feel comfortable setting foot outside of Australia. Particularly now that Martin and Hewitt had returned to the States.

After a few minutes, Cru cupped my cheek and I looked into his eyes.

My breath caught when I asked how long he'd be able to stay at the exact moment he asked when I thought I'd be able to leave.

"I'm not sure," I answered first.

He nodded, but his hurt was palpable.

"What about you?" I asked.

Cru shrugged. "I'm not sure, either. It depends on when and what I hear from Bit. My ticket is open-ended."

I wished I saw that as a good thing, but it didn't feel that way. All it meant was he could leave tomorrow if it became necessary.

"Your dad seems…"

I waited for him to finish, and when he didn't, I said, "Better?"

"No, since I have nothing to base it on. I guess it's just that I don't see…"

"See what, Cru?" I snapped, irritated that he wasn't finishing his sentences.

"What you can do for him that isn't already being done."

I nodded. "There's more to my being here."

"The board, you mean?"

I eased from his arms and sat up. "What I mean is there is someone working very hard to steal my family's business away while my dad is in hospital, recovering from a stroke brought on by the same person's actions. If the bastard is successful, it would mean losing everything my parents worked their whole lives for."

I didn't care for the way he was looking at me. In fact, it reminded me of Beau.

"You think I'm being melodramatic." I stood and went into the bathroom, where I knew a robe hung on the back of the door.

When I returned, Cru was sitting up with his legs dangling over the side of the bed. The sheet covered the lower half of his body.

"Don't put words in my mouth, Daphne."

"What choice do I have when you won't just say what you're thinking?"

"I'm asking simple questions. Why are you getting angry?"

I sat beside him but kept my arms folded. "You're right and I'm sorry."

"Come here." Cru shifted us both so we lay on the bed, looking into each other's eyes. He put his hand on my leg and lifted it so it rested over his thigh, causing the robe to gape open. He covered one exposed breast with his palm and leaned forward to kiss me. "I've missed you so much. The last thing I want to do is argue."

"I feel the same, and again, I'm sorry."

"I want us to be together, Daphne. Like we were before. Living together, working in the vineyards, spending all night making love—it was a dream come true."

"But—"

"Please let me finish."

"Apologies, again. Go on."

"For now, you need to stay here and I need to return to Los Caballeros. We both have obligations to fulfill. I just hope that when things are sorted out with Cullen House, you can come home."

I knew what he meant, and a few weeks ago, I would've agreed that Los Caballeros was my home. However, I didn't see his commitment to his family's business as being temporary. Why did he automatically assume mine would be any different?

"I have to see this through," I said, looking everywhere but in his eyes.

"I know you do."

"You do?"

His head cocked, and his eyes scrunched. "Why are you asking?"

"What if seeing it through means I have to remain in Perth? What if this is home for me?"

He looked crestfallen, but we had to accept that may be my reality.

"Cru?"

"Is that what you want?"

"The point I'm trying to make is that I don't know. I won't until we can move beyond the impasse we're at now."

"We?"

"Sorry. Cullen House."

He rolled to his back, and I removed my leg from over his body.

"What do you want, Daphne? To be a winemaker or the CEO of a corporation? To be in an office every day or out in the vineyard?"

"You're being unfair."

"Am I? Before you respond, I have one more question for you, and I want you to think about it before you answer."

I nodded.

"Do you want to be my wife, Daph?"

I rolled to my back like he had, looked up at the ceiling, and closed my eyes. Of course I wanted to marry him. I also wanted to work in the vines, spend my days in the sun, and make wine. But like him, I had a familial responsibility I couldn't just turn my back on.

"You're choosing Los Caballeros over me."

He propped himself up on his elbow. "Is that the way you see it?"

"What if I asked you to leave it behind, move here, and help me run Cullen House?"

He sighed. "Answer my question, Daphne. It's really the only thing that truly matters right now."

"I do want to be your wife, Cru…"

"But?"

I was about to say the hardest thing I'd ever had to in my life. Once I spoke the words, there'd be no taking them back, no way for us to continue on together. I knew that. Yet, I had to be honest. "I don't see how it will be possible. Our lives are on opposite sides of the world."

He sat up abruptly and turned his back to me.

"Cru?"

He took a deep breath and let it out in a shudder.

"Talk to me," I said.

He shook his head. "I can't."

"This doesn't have to be the end. We can work something out, can't we?"

When he looked over his shoulder at me, the tears streaming down his cheeks were my undoing. "Can't we?" I repeated. My sobs clogged my throat, and I couldn't say anything more, even after he left the room, then returned fully dressed.

"You said you didn't see how it could be possible, Daphne. So how are we supposed to work something out? Which is it?"

"I don't know."

"Neither do I." He took another deep breath, looked up at the ceiling, then at me. "Goodbye, Daphne."

I gasped. "You're *leaving*?"

"I don't see any reason to stay."

I hugged myself, wishing so desperately that Cru and I were in each other's arms instead. "Your ring. It's in my bedroom. I'll just get it—"

"Don't. It's not mine, it's yours."

"I can't keep it, Cru."

"I don't want it, Daphne."

I sat on the bed, crying for several minutes, expecting he'd return and we'd at least talk about when he planned to leave.

When he didn't, I went looking for him. The front door of the guesthouse was slightly ajar, so I went outside.

One of the housekeepers walked past. "Have you seen a man, quite tall, dark brown hair?"

"Yes, miss."

"Where is he?"

"He left a few minutes ago."

My eyes scrunched. "What do you mean?"

"A car picked him up, and he left."

I nodded once and retreated inside before I broke into shattering sobs. As many times as Beau and I had ended things between us, I'd never felt like I did now. I doubled over in pain, crying harder as I realized my heart had just broken.

When I showed up at the rehab center a couple of hours later, both my parents appeared puzzled.

"Is Cru resting?" my mum asked.

I shook my head, keeping my eyes focused on hers, knowing that if I looked at my dad instead, I'd break down. "He had to leave."

The sound that came from my father was one of the worst I'd ever heard. He wailed, repeating the word "no" again and again.

"It's okay, Dad," I said, rushing over to him. "The harvest. He couldn't stay long."

He shook his head. "No," he repeated, grabbing my wrist when I turned to leave, not wanting to upset him.

"Dad, please…"

"No…Daphne…*No*. Can't stay." He closed his eyes and dropped his head, shaking it vehemently. "Go home."

"This is home, Dad."

My mum, who was crying as hard as me, got up and left the room.

I knelt beside my father and grasped his hands with mine. "You need me here. I can't leave."

Tears streamed down his cheeks. *"Don't want."*

I rested my head on his lap, and both of us cried.

23

Cru

Instead of going straight to the airport, I asked the driver to take me to the harbor. I sat in a bar, looking out over the water, waiting, hoping, and praying my phone would ring and Daphne would ask me to come back.

After a couple of hours, I knew two things: she wasn't going to call, and if I kept drinking, I'd never be allowed on a plane.

I ordered food, switched from bourbon to water, then called another car service. While I waited, I booked a flight to the States. I was able to get a seat on one that left later tonight. Rather than stopping in Sydney, I'd travel through Manila. With the layover, it would take me over twenty-four hours to get home. But time didn't matter. I was leaving behind the woman I'd loved most of my life. Nothing mattered now. Nothing ever would again.

Instead of asking anyone to pick me up, I took a car service from the San Luis Obispo airport home. When I arrived, I paid the driver and walked into a house I no longer wanted to live in.

Unable to bear the idea of lying on either bed where Daphne and I had made love, I went up to the third floor and locked the door behind me when I reached the top of the landing. I hadn't allowed myself to cry since I broke down while still with Daphne. Now, there was nothing to stop me. I could cry for days, and no one would even know I was here.

When I opened my eyes, it was dark outside and someone was banging on the locked door.

"Go away!" I shouted.

"Open the door, Cru."

Rather than my brother's, who I'd expected it to be, the voice coming from the opposite side was that of my best friend, Beau. The last person in the world I wanted to talk to right now.

"I'll break it down if you don't unlock it."

I'd tell him to fuck off, but I knew Beau would follow through with his threat, and then I'd have to replace a broken door at the same time as finding a way to heal my broken heart.

I flipped the lock and sat on the sofa with my arms folded.

"Why are you back?" he demanded before telling me I looked like shit.

"You can leave," I responded without looking up at him.

"Why aren't you in Australia?" he shouted.

"None of your fucking business," I yelled back.

"Where's Daphne?"

This time, I didn't bother answering. "Why are you here?" I asked instead.

He sat in one of the chairs that faced me. "We all are."

"What the fuck does that mean?"

"Bit called a meeting, asking Los Caballeros to help out."

I scrubbed my face. "You can't be serious."

"Do you really think he'd let you leave without bringing in reinforcements?"

"*Let* me leave? He and the rest of the crew threatened to go on strike if I didn't."

Beau laughed.

"It isn't funny, asshole."

He got up and went into the small kitchen, opening and closing doors. "Don't you have anything to drink?"

"I came up here to be left alone, not to entertain."

"Come on. Let's go."

I cocked my head and looked up at him. "You go."

"If I do, you'll probably lock the door again."

"You got that right."

He walked over, sat in the chair, and stared at me, but didn't say anything.

"What?"

He shook his head.

"You're a dick." I got up and went into the bedroom. The asshole followed me.

"What happened with Daphne?"

"I already told you it's none of your business."

"No, you said that when I asked why you weren't in Australia."

"Ditto."

"I suppose I could just call her and ask."

"She'll tell you as much as I have." I put the pillow over my face.

"I take it the engagement is off?"

I moved the pillow. "Were there any knives in the drawers out there?"

"Why?"

"Stab me. It'll have the same effect."

"So why are you here?"

"I asked Daphne if she wanted to be my wife. She responded she didn't see how it would be possible since our lives were on opposite sides of the world."

His eyes scrunched. "That doesn't sound like her."

I glared at him. "Fuck off, Beau."

"Why can't you trade off? It couldn't be more ideal, really. The seasons are opposite. You could be there in our winter, and she could be here in hers."

"Because Daphne isn't a winemaker when she's there. She's the acting CEO of a huge conglomerate."

He nodded. "My dad said it isn't looking good. She—they—may lose Cullen House."

"When she told me she feared that may happen, she didn't give me the chance to respond before asking if I thought she was being melodramatic."

He sighed and looked at the wall behind me.

"What?"

"I used to say that to her."

"Well, that's fair. She got mad at me for something you used to say. Nice."

"So, you left?"

"Obviously, or I wouldn't be here."

"I'm tired of your dickish attitude. You can stop now. I'm only trying to help."

"Why?"

Beau leaned forward and rested his elbows on his knees. "Because I love both of you. Because you belong together, and I can't believe that you, of all people, would give up so easily."

"She gave me no choice." I slumped onto the sofa and shut my eyes. "Would you just go away and leave me alone?"

"What was the last thing she said to you?"

"Again, it's none of your business."

He raised a brow, and his nostrils flared. "Just tell me."

"She said the ring I gave her was in her bedroom and she'd go and get it. I told her I didn't want it."

"Then what?"

"I left."

"This is the part I don't get. You knew things here were taken care of. You could've stayed and tried to work things out."

"Why? I can't leave Los Cab. She can't leave Cullen House. She was right to say it can't work."

"Cru, how much money do you have?"

I opened my eyes and raised my head. "I don't know."

"Millions?"

I shrugged.

"Billions?"

"Maybe not plural."

"You could buy a plane and hire a pilot. Or Daphne could. She's probably worth more than you are. You could fly to Australia as much as you wanted and vice versa, at least until she's able to work things out with Cullen House. Or until her dad is well enough to return himself."

I shook my head. "He's not good, Beau. He can hardly speak."

"That's what my father said."

"I love Daphne. I've never loved anyone else and doubt that I ever will, but I can't do what you're suggesting, Beau. I can't be away from Los Cab on a regular basis. I can't live part of the year in Australia."

He stood and walked to the door. "Then, you don't really love her."

I stood too. "That's bullshit. Just because you couldn't commit—"

"Stop right there." He stalked over to me. "I did commit. I gave up my life in California to be with Sam in New York. Maybe you're right that I never committed to Daphne, but I never felt for her the way I do for Sam."

"Congratulations. You're the bigger man. Now, leave."

To my surprise, that's exactly what he did. His words, however, stuck with me. Maybe I could do what he'd suggested and look into getting a plane. On the other hand, once the harvest was over, I could buy a one-way ticket like I had before. Only this time, I wouldn't leave until I convinced Daphne I loved her and would do anything to be with her.

24

Daphne

It had been a month since Cru returned to California after being in Australia for less than twenty-four hours.

In that time, the only progress I'd made with the board was finding an addendum to Cullen House's original articles of corporation stating that the entire board must vote on the removal or replacement of the chairman. Five minutes after reading it, then confirming there was no addendum to the addendum negating it, I rang Martin Barrett and Hewitt Ridge, asking them to become "unavailable" for a vote. Both men agreed to my request. At the very least, it would buy me more time to figure out a way to get rid of Dorian.

Also in the time since Cru left, my father had exceeded his doctor's expectations on his recovery. He could get around on his feet, albeit with either a cane or, if he was fatigued, a walker. And he no longer had signs of facial paralysis.

He'd returned home but hadn't yet gone into the office, and neither my mum nor I thought it was a good idea for him to do so.

He still had rehab three times a week, but instead of him traveling to the office, he'd arranged for the therapists to come to the house.

While his speech wasn't one hundred percent, he was perfectly capable of arguing with me, which he did on a daily basis.

Every morning over coffee, the first thing he'd say after "good morning" was that it was time for me to return to California. I'd respond that I'd leave when and if I wanted to, but for now, I planned to remain in Perth until he was able to return to his position as CEO.

By the end of breakfast, he would've said I had neither the experience nor the education to run "his" business, after which I'd remind him he'd only gotten a bachelor's degree, whereas I had a master's.

That he also felt the need to remind me that my passion was for making wine, not selling it, only worsened the ache in my chest.

All the while, my mum would shake her head and laugh at the two of us.

I never returned to my childhood bedroom after Cru left. Instead, I stayed in the other of the two guest-houses. I couldn't bear to set foot in the one he and I had briefly shared.

I was desperate to know how the harvest was going at Los Cab, but I'd not contact anyone and ask. I hadn't heard a single word from Cru since the day he left and didn't want it to get back to him that I'd been in contact with his family or employees.

If anyone, including my father, had asked if I was enjoying my life, which mainly revolved around Cullen House, I would've had to lie or admit I hated nearly every minute of it. Some might say that, in itself, would be reason enough to return to the States, but until I fulfilled the promise I'd made to myself to stick it out until the turmoil with the board was over and Steve Dorian was booted out on his ear, I was staying put.

"Daphne? May I interrupt you?" my mother asked when she found me sitting in the sunroom reading something on my laptop.

"Of course. What is it, Mum?"

"You have a visitor. That's to say, we have visitors. Many, in fact."

I rested against the cushion of my chair and studied her. "What do you mean?"

"Well, to begin, Beau Barrett is on his way here to see you."

My heart sank. For the briefest of moments, I hoped she'd say Cru had returned. "And the others?"

"It seems the entirety of Los Caballeros has arrived in Perth."

I was even more confused. My brow furrowed, and I shook my head. "I'm not following."

"I'll explain," said Beau. He leaned in and kissed my mother's cheek. "Good to see you, Beatrice," he said.

The two embraced, then my mum left the room.

"This is some greeting," he said when I remained seated with my arms folded.

"I'm mad at you."

He knelt down and nudged me. "That's nothing new."

"Why are you here, Beau?"

"Press and I flew the Viejos here."

I rubbed my temples with my index fingers. "I feel a migraine coming on. Wait, it's already here." I nudged him back.

"It's time you learned about what, or who, Los Caballeros is outside of the estate and winery."

I set my laptop aside and stood. "I'm not interested."

"Hmm. Well, then, I suppose you'll have to leave."

"Argh." I clenched my fists at my sides. "If anyone is vacating the premises, it's you."

"Eventually, I will, but not until I tell you everything I came to say."

"This is a nightmare. There's no other explanation."

Beau stood. "All I'm asking you to do is listen."

"Go on."

"Have a seat."

I thought to remind him that he'd just said all I had to do was listen, which didn't require I be seated, but figured that would just prolong whatever was happening.

When I sat in a chair by the window, he pulled one of the others beside it and sat next to me.

I covered my face with my hands, wishing I could stop myself from asking, but I had to. "Beau, before you get started, is Cru here?"

"Sorry, Daph. He's not."

I took a deep breath and squared my shoulders. "Let's get on with it. The sooner you're finished, the sooner you can be on your way."

"You're not very nice."

"I learned it from you," I snapped.

He raised a brow and nodded. "That's probably true."

"How's it going?" my mum asked from behind us.

"I haven't gotten started yet," Beau told her.

"I see. Well, I've brought water, lemonade, wine, and bourbon. Let me know if there's anything you'd fancy instead."

"Thank you," said Beau.

It wasn't fair of me to take my frustration with him out on my mother. "Yes, thanks, Mum," I said over my shoulder, wondering why she felt it necessary to include bourbon at this hour.

"I told you that Press and I flew the Viejos here," Beau began.

I nodded.

"Do you know who I was referring to?"

I spoke fluent Spanish, so I knew what the word meant. "Old people?"

He chuckled. "They might take exception to the translation, but they chose the name; I didn't."

"Get. On. With. It."

"Okay, okay."

I listened as Beau spun a tale about a secret society that had been founded centuries ago in Spain. They called themselves Los Caballeros, and at one time, they'd been more marauders than what they were now.

"I wouldn't say the present-day organization is akin to Robin Hood. However, we are best described as good-guy vigilantes."

"We?"

Beau nodded. "I'm a member, as is Press. So are Brix, Ridge, Zin, Bones, Snapper, Kick, and Cru. And, as of last month, Bit."

"And the Viejos?"

"Your father is one, as is mine."

I shook my head. "You're saying my father has been a member of a secret society that neither my mum nor I knew anything about?"

"Your mother knew."

"Why does she, and I don't?"

"Because it's a secret only shared with the love of a caballero's life."

"Won't you lose your membership card for telling me?"

He smiled. "Nah. I've got Cru's proxy."

To my chagrin, my eyes filled with tears. "This isn't funny, Beau. In fact, you're cruel." I stood and walked toward the door.

"Don't leave, Daphne. The last thing I meant to do was hurt you."

"I'd hate to see what you'd do if you did. Use a knife maybe?"

He chuckled—again.

"There's nothing about this that's laughable."

"You're right. It's just that Cru said the same thing."

"*Beau!* Why are you doing this?"

He got up, walked over, and pulled me into his arms. "Because I love him and I love you and this impasse must end."

"What does any of this have to do with your vigilante group?"

He led me over to the sofa rather than the chairs where we'd been seated a minute ago and pulled me down beside him.

"The answer is two-fold but designed to accomplish the same thing."

I opened my mouth to speak, but Beau held up his hand.

"If you stop interrupting me, I'll tell you."

I shut it and nodded.

"The men in the other room—some you know quite well and others I think you've met at least once in your life—are here to help your father in a continuation of what you started. Brilliant, by the way, that you asked Hewitt and my father to make themselves unavailable to vote your father off the board. It bought valuable time. As far as what I mean to accomplish, my ultimate goal is to convince you to return to California."

"I can't."

"What if Steve Dorian was completely out of the picture, as were the board members who've sided with him? Then would you go?"

"It's too late. Cru walked out, and I haven't heard a word from him since he left."

"Count yourself lucky. No one I know *wants* to talk to him."

"Don't, Beau. I love him."

"Yes, Daphne, I know you do. And he loves you. The two of you belong together."

"You asked if I'd go if Steve Dorian was out of the picture. How do you intend to make that happen?"

"Not me, the Viejos."

I rolled my eyes. "How was it I was with you for so long? You are one of the most maddening people I've ever known."

Beau took my hand in his. "We kept each other company while I was waiting for Sam and you were waiting for Cru."

I wriggled from his grasp. "Back to the Viejos."

"I'll let them tell you. But after they do, if things are the way I said, will you fly home with Press and me?"

"I can't answer that."

"There she is," said Martin when we walked out of the sunroom to where they were gathered. He looked at Beau. "Did you tell her?"

He nodded. "She knows, but since she speaks fluent Spanish, she keeps referring to you as the old guys instead of the Viejos."

"I do not." I punched his arm and looked around the room at those gathered, happy to see Tryst was here, along with Hewitt Ridge and George Norman.

I recognized many of the others, but since, as Beau had said, I'd met some only once in my life, I couldn't recall all their names. There was one other, closer to my age, who looked vaguely familiar, but I couldn't place him. My mind was already reeling.

"Did Beau tell you what we learned about Steve Dorian?" Hewitt asked.

"I thought I'd let you tell her."

"Good. Well, as it turns out, the Dorians are related to the family who owns another of Australia's wine conglomerates—the Palmer Group."

I recognized the name. The company was well known, not just in Australia but around the world. Their organization rivaled Cullen House in both size and annual sales.

"How did he get on our board?" I asked.

"He went to great pains to conceal the affiliation," said Martin.

"I have no doubt his plan was to figure out a way to sabotage Cullen House after he succeeded in getting me, Hewitt, and Martin off the board," said my father. "Then undervalue it and sell it to the Palmer Group."

"Is that legal?" I asked.

"Not in the slightest," said one of the other men. "By the way, Daphne, I'm Michael Oliver, if you don't recognize me."

"Sorry. I do. I'm just struggling with remembering all your names."

Hewitt nudged Martin. "I told you we should wear badges."

Beau's father rolled his eyes. "Get on with it, Michael."

"Several years ago, Australia passed what's called the EFI Act, which criminalized corporate espionage. Penalties can result in prison time as well as millions of dollars in damages."

"What we're working on now is finding links between the board members Dorian appointed and the Palmer Group," said Martin. "Even if we're unable to, once he's gone, it's likely they'll resign anyway."

The younger man stepped forward. "Daphne, I don't know if you remember me, but I'm your cousin, err, Noah Cullen. I go by NC to avoid confusion."

I did remember my father's brother's son—who'd been named for my dad like Hewitt Ridge's oldest son had—but it had been years since I last saw him.

"I've been working for Cullen House since I graduated from university."

"NC has been working undercover, if you will, to gather information about the board members Dorian appointed," said Martin.

Part of me wondered why I hadn't been informed prior to now, and another part was just happy to know there were others at Cullen House in my father's corner.

My eyes scrunched. "What's the next step?"

My father got up and, with the help of a walker, crossed the room and stood in front of me. "I love you with all my heart, Daphne. Your mother and I have appreciated everything you've done for us—for me, in particular—but it's time for you to go home."

My eyes filled with tears, and I leaned forward and rested my head on his shoulder. "I don't know where that is anymore," I whispered.

"Of course you do."

I shook my head. "What if he no longer wants me?"

Beau rubbed my shoulder. "Trust me, Daph. He does. He's just too stubborn to do anything about it."

My mum walked over and stood beside my dad. "If we thought for one minute you'd be happy here, we'd be thrilled for you to stay. But you won't be. Follow your dreams, sweetheart. Better put, return to them."

I looked around the room and stopped when my eyes met Tryst's.

"The path is right in front of you, Daphne. All you have to do is take it."

I closed my eyes and nodded, remembering the day he'd brought me to the temple at his ranch. As I was walking in, he'd said those same words to me.

I turned to my father. "What about Cullen House?"

"I intend to return to work as soon as the doctors clear me. And NC will be taking over as vice president."

I glanced at my cousin, then at my mother, then back at my father. Again, I was irritated that I hadn't been informed of any of this, but had I left California and returned to Perth to take over my parents' business? No. I came because my dad had a stroke. The only reason I'd gotten involved at all was because I inadvertently learned about Steve Dorian when he called to demand I meet with him and the board after likely learning I held my father's power of attorney.

That set forth a chain of events that could only be described as a trainwreck.

"May I have some privacy to speak with my parents?" I asked, looking around the room.

"Come with me," said Beau, ushering the men into another part of the house. For the first time since I laid eyes on him today, I was grateful he was here. Beau and I had history, and we were friends—good ones. Later, after I'd spoken to my mum and dad, I'd apologize and thank him for being here. His only agenda was to help, and in doing so, he'd left Sam in the States. I felt horrible for the way I'd treated him.

I motioned to the table, and the three of us took a seat. "Dad, are you sure this is what you want to do?"

"If you mean going back to work, then yes. As far as NC is concerned…" He sighed and rested his chin on his hand. "Daphne, this isn't where you belong. Your mum and I love you so much, and we miss you an equal amount, but neither of us can stand by and watch you throw away your chance at happiness for something none of us ever intended."

"But—"

My mother put her hand on mine. "Let him finish, sweetheart."

"I've known for years that you had no interest in running Cullen House, and it never bothered me. Your mother and I just want you to be happy."

Tears ran down my cheeks, and my mother squeezed my fingers. "For the last several months, your dad and I have talked about selling so we could retire and spend more time in California. Now might not be the time to do so, given whatever damage Dorian may have done; however, it's still an idea. In the meantime, NC will handle most of the day-to-day things your father looked over. He's never once asked us for anything, by the way. In fact, your father wasn't aware he'd applied for a job until HR contacted him and said they'd received an application from someone with his same name."

"He's earned this, darling," my dad added.

I nodded.

"Your dream is to live and work in the vines," he continued. "It always has been. As you reminded me every morning, you do have a master's degree in both viticulture and enology."

I chuckled. "And you reminded me I wasn't cut out for running the business."

He smiled. "This is about more than your dream of making wine, sweetheart. It's about a life with the man you love. I cannot sit by and let you turn your back on what makes everything we do worthwhile." He reached across the table and rested his hand on top of my mum's and mine. "Love, Daphne, and family. It's all that matters. Now, *go home*."

"Okay. I'll go."

"Excellent. Now, hurry and pack," Beau said from behind me.

"Eavesdropper," I muttered.

"Listen, if we don't leave in the next two hours, we won't be there in time for the Wicked Winemakers bachelor auction," he said.

"I thought you were engaged or married or something. Are you really going to make Sam bid on you?"

"I'm not the bachelor, Daph. Cru is."

25

Cru

"But you promised!" my sister shouted at me.

"No, Alex, I didn't. In fact, I never agreed to be in the auction this year or any other. The difference now is I don't care what you threaten me with. I'm finally putting my foot down. I'm not doing it."

"You're already listed in the program."

"Say it was a typo."

She folded her arms. "You have to be there anyway to represent Los Cab. What's the big deal about being in the auction if you're already there?"

"Because someone will bid on me, and I'll have to spend a lot of money on a fancy date with a person I don't want to know."

"It's for charity, Cru. All the money goes to the children's hospital. Think about that."

I shook my head. "You know damn well that I always make a donation anyway. A sizable one."

"Will you double it this year?"

My eyes scrunched. "I will on one condition."

"Name it."

"You never ask me to be in this stupid auction again."

She drummed her fingers on the counter. "It isn't stupid."

"Alex…" I warned.

"All right. I'll never ask again."

"Wait. You said I was already in the program. What was the date?"

"Hot-air ballooning over the vineyards, followed by dinner in the old winery."

"Get out of here, Al."

She cocked her head. "What did I say?"

"Nothing. Just go."

"God, you're a moody asshole lately."

I pointed to the door.

"All right, I'm leaving. Jeez."

Hot fucking air ballooning over the vineyard. Why did that have to be what Alex had come up with?

I had a tuxedo. All the men in my family did. As one of the largest wineries on the Central Coast, we were required to attend all sorts of black-tie functions, most of which were fundraisers. None were bigger than the Wicked Winemakers' Ball, the highlight of the post-harvest season. My sister was appointed chair of the event a few years ago and quadrupled the money the event raised by adding a bachelor auction.

I'd been coerced to participate since the year it started, as had the rest of my brothers and my fellow *caballeros*. Brix and Ridge were the first to get married, thus they no longer qualified to be auctioned off. Beau, his brother, Press, and Zin were also off the market enough that Alex left them alone.

Given the number of eligible men was dwindling, my sister had become more of a pest about participation. Snapper and Kick, who'd used their travel on the rodeo circuit more than once as an excuse to miss it, were here this year. New to the auction were guys I remembered being kids, but were now old enough to be bid on. The other new "kid" on the auction block this year was Bit.

On the one hand, I was pissed at Alex for forcing him to do it. On the other, it was one more indicator of "normalcy" in my brother's life.

I got out of the shower, dried off, and got dressed. As I looked in the mirror, attempting to get the bow tied right, I studied my reflection. There was more gray in my hair than I remembered there being even as recently as last week. The bags under my eyes looked worse, and the wrinkles on my forehead were deeper. Frankly, even I had to admit I looked like shit.

In previous auctions, I hadn't cared who'd bid on me. I only owed the winner one date, and most years, the woman was someone I'd known since childhood.

The idea of spending time with a female other than Daphne—even as friends—still turned my stomach. When I wasn't feeling nauseated, I ached. I left the bathroom and sat on the end of the bed. I pulled the tie from around my neck and tossed it on the floor. Was it really necessary I wear one? I wouldn't be getting up on stage.

It had occurred to me that, once I was at the venue, Alex might attempt to call me up anyway. I'd already decided that if she did, I'd get up, push my chair in, and leave. If she thought she could trick me by putting me on the spot, she'd have a hefty dose of humiliation headed her way.

"Cru?" I heard my brother call my name from the other room.

"I'm here, Bit," I said, joining him in the living room.

He held up his tie. "Can you help me with this damned thing?" What I noticed more than his frustration over an article of clothing no one liked wearing was his underlying happiness. It wasn't something I saw or felt from him that often.

"Looking forward to tonight?" I asked.

He shrugged. "I hope someone bids on me."

"You're kidding, right?" I thought back to Daphne saying that, of all the Avila brothers, he was the most "muscular." I knew she meant more than that. He was also the best looking. "Your bid might be the highest of the night."

"You think so?" he asked as I finished tying the bow, then straightened.

"I sure do," I said, resting my hands on his shoulders. "I'm proud of you, and I love you, Bit."

"I love you too, Cru."

I turned around and went into the kitchen to pour myself a glass of wine but also to hide the tears in my eyes. I hated how fucking emotional I was lately almost as much as I hated the pain in my heart whenever I thought about Daph, which was pretty much every waking hour.

"You ready to go?" he asked.

"Sure—" I stopped myself from saying I wanted to get this night over with. It wasn't fair for my depression to affect my brother. He'd battled enough of it on his own through the years. After he was attacked, it seemed worse.

When we walked in and made our way to our table that was always positioned in the center of the room, I was stunned to see Beau there with Sam. Press was in attendance too, with his wife, Luisa.

"I didn't expect you guys tonight," I said, walking up to embrace them one by one.

"The gang is all here, from what I've heard," said Beau, motioning behind me.

I glanced over my shoulder and saw my oldest brother walking toward me with his hand on his wife's back. "Brix," I said, meeting them halfway. "Hey, Addy."

"Hi, Cru."

"How are you feeling?" I asked.

"Hopeful there's something spicy enough on the menu tonight that this little nugget decides it's finally time to make an appearance." She patted her stomach, which looked like it was about to burst.

"If not, we can always get my ma to make you something afterwards. I hear she's got a recipe that guarantees to induce labor." A couple of months after they moved to Mexico, Brix called with the news that Addy was pregnant. It seemed hard to believe that enough time had passed and she was about to give birth.

She smacked Brix's arm. "Why am I hearing this now and from your brother? My due date was a week ago."

"Sorry, honey," he said, looking sheepish and rubbing her shoulders.

"You're not forgiven."

I raised a brow at him, then laughed when she brushed past me to say hello to Sam. "You're whipped, man."

"I hear it gets worse during labor. I've been building up to it."

"I didn't know you'd be in town."

He nodded. "Thought it best that the baby be delivered here, with Ma and Addy's mother. The hospital in Álamos is nice, but with all the money Alex raises for the local ones, we both decided we'd be more comfortable here."

"Wait. How long have you been in town?"

"Just got here last night, but if she had gone into labor sooner, the jet was on standby."

That didn't sound like a very smart plan to me, but what did I know? The closest I'd ever get to babies was by being their uncle.

I grabbed the bottle from the center of Los Cab's table and poured us each a glass. "Did you hear Bit's on the block tonight?" I asked.

He waved the program in front of me. "I'm surprised you agreed this year."

I sneered. "Alex did it without asking me, and when I found out, I told her if she tried to get me up there, I'd humiliate her in ways she couldn't even imagine."

"Like what?"

"I don't know. I haven't come up with anything other than walking out."

"She didn't call your bluff, then?"

"Not yet anyway."

"I hate to tell you, but the brat is making a beeline for us now."

"Hi, Brix," she said, kissing our brother's cheek before turning to me. "There's been a development. You, um, *have* to be in the auction tonight."

I looked around me to see who was close enough to hear what I was about to say, then leaned in. "No fucking way, Al. I told you what would happen if you pulled this shit."

"But there is a really good reason. I mean, *really* good."

"No, and if you don't drop it, I'm walking out of here right now."

Her eyes opened wide. *"You can't."*

"Try me."

I watched as she turned and made eye contact with Beau. He shook his head, then went back to his conversation with Sam and Addy. What was that all about?

"I have to ask one more time. I'll get down on my knees and beg if I have to."

"You can crawl around on the floor all night, Alex, and I'm still not going to do it. There is no way in hell I will set foot on the stage tonight. *No possible way.*"

Her eyes scrunched, and I could tell there was more she wanted to say, but talked herself out of it.

"What was that look between you and my sister?" I approached Beau and asked.

"She asked for my assistance."

I nodded, but my gut told me there was more to it. However, I knew that my best course of action was to not engage Alex again tonight. She'd only see it as an opening to keep trying to get me on stage.

"Hey, I want to apologize for how much of an asshole I've been lately."

Beau raised a brow. "Lately?"

"You still have me outnumbered in collective days of being a douche by a few years."

He shook his head. "I won't argue with you on that one. Being with Sam, though, has changed me for the better in ways I never dreamed possible."

Brix approached and put his hand on my shoulder. "That's what comes when you're in love with the right woman."

"As I've heard."

"So, what are you going to do about it?"

I hadn't planned on telling anyone other than Bit, but I knew the two would keep after me all night if I didn't divulge my intentions. "I'm on a flight out on Monday, traveling to Perth."

Like the look that had passed between Beau and Alex, I caught a similar one between my oldest brother and my best friend.

"What's up?" I asked.

Beau put his hand on my other shoulder. "Nothing, man. Just glad to hear it."

I didn't believe him, but it didn't matter what they thought. I had to go to Australia. Even if Daphne couldn't leave, we'd figure it out. We had to. I'd loved her most of my life, and now that I knew how it felt to have her love me back, it wasn't something I could live without.

26

Daphne

"What do you mean he's not participating?" I practically screeched at Alex.

"He's refusing. In fact, he said if I didn't let it go, he'd leave now."

I sat on a chair in the office where Beau had brought me when I arrived, saying the element of surprise would work best in this case. "He won't make a scene if you bid on him. You know he won't," he'd said when he convinced me to do this.

Now what?

I glanced at Alex, who had a look on her face I'd come to recognize. She was plotting something.

"What?" I asked.

She looked up at me. "I have an idea."

I raised a brow and cocked my head. "Again, what?"

"What if we…"

27

Cru

One of the reasons I drove myself to the ball tonight was so I wouldn't have too much to drink. We were over two hours in, and I'd had one glass of wine, along with a four-course meal. The last served was dessert, which I looked forward to every year. My favorite was always the banana-chocolate cake, which looked and tasted like nothing I ever imagined it would. According to the description on the menu, it was made of crunchy almond praline, chocolate mousse, and banana confit. I had no idea what the last thing was, only that it tasted fantastic.

"Here we go," said Brix, motioning to the stage, where the auction would take place.

I groaned, then reminded myself the main reason I was here was to make sure everything went okay with Bit. I'd gone so far as to ask a couple of the women I knew would be here tonight to bid on him. In both instances, when I offered to cover the cost, they said they'd already planned to bid on him. While I was relieved they were, I couldn't help but feel anxious. Bit had always been uncomfortable being the center of attention, and in this case, he would be in ways far exceeding anything he'd experienced before.

I took a deep breath, glad my older brother was beside me, knowing he was as anxious as I was that it all go okay.

Alex went through her usual over-the-top introductions when each new bachelor came on stage, trying to drive the bids up so she'd bring in more money than she had in years past.

Since I was scheduled to be last, that honor would fall on Bit since he was right before me.

Surprisingly, he handled it better than I ever had. He didn't make a spectacle of himself like Zin always had, nor did he shy away from it. He smiled with an air of calm confidence.

"He's doing great," Brix leaned over and said.

"He sure is."

Bids were the highest of the night, driven up by one of the two women I'd spoken to. The winner, though, was someone I hadn't talked to. Eberly Warwick upped her final offer by five grand, a collective gasp went through the audience, and when Alex lowered the gavel, saying she'd won, the crowd got to their feet and cheered.

The whole thing couldn't have gone better if I had staged it.

"Okay, everyone, bear with me. We have one more date to auction," I heard my sister say.

"Fuck," I said under my breath, pushing my chair back—or trying to. When I looked over my shoulder, Beau, Press, and Zin stood directly behind me. "What the hell?" I said, looking at Beau.

"You can't leave."

"Watch me."

"Shh. Just listen." He pointed to the stage.

"Ladies, I know this is unconventional, but we're introducing something new this year. My brother Cru has graciously set aside his date so we could bring our first ever bachelorette on stage."

Muttering, followed by cheers, went around the room, and Alex cleared her throat.

"This bachelor-*ette*"—she emphasized the last syllable—"is wine-industry royalty, not just here on the Central Coast but around the world. Gentlemen, the date you see listed on the program is what's being offered. A fabulous hot-air-balloon ride over the vineyards, at sunset, I might add. Followed by dinner in the original winery on the Los Caballeros estate." She looked around the room until her eyes settled on me. "Who wants to start the bidding? Can I get five grand?"

"Who is she?" someone shouted.

"Right! How could I have forgotten to introduce our grand finale guest—Daphne Cullen."

Alex's eyes bored into mine even though we were several feet apart. Her gaze never wavered, even when I looked away.

Bids were coming from all around me, but I didn't know what they were. All I could focus on was Daphne. She looked more beautiful than I'd ever seen.

The blue-green sequined dress she wore hugged her curves, accentuating her breasts, slim waist, and her perfect ass. The idea that any other man here would ever touch any part of her body had me slam my chair back and stand.

"Twenty thousand going once," Alex said, looking at me.

Someone—I wasn't sure who—put a paddle in my hand, and I raised it. "Thirty," I shouted.

"Forty!" Beau said from behind me.

"Fifty!" I countered. I'd stare him down, but there was no way I'd take my eyes off the woman I loved with all my heart.

"Fifty going once..." Alex slammed the gavel down without finishing the call for bids. "Sold to my brother, Cru."

Applause came from around the room as I made my way to the stage. It wasn't customary, but I couldn't wait. Once there, I hoisted myself up, took Daphne in my arms, and kissed her like a man possessed. She put her hand on my cheek, and I felt the coolness of the ring on her finger.

"You're wearing your engagement ring," I said, resting my forehead against hers. "Does that mean you want to be my wife, Daphne?"

"Yes, Cru. More than anything. I love you."

I smiled. "And I love you."

I kissed her again, then led her toward the back of the stage. Rather than return to the table, I kept going until we reached the rear entrance. There, I gathered her in my arms and carried her the rest of the way to where I'd parked.

"Where are we going?" she asked when I set her on her feet so I could unlock the door.

"Home."

Epilogue

Cru

"It's not too late to change your mind. We can always do this in Australia," I said to Daphne the night before our wedding.

"Then we'd have to charter a plane to fly everyone who's here, there."

"We can do that."

Daph shook her head. "I cannot imagine a setting more perfect. Los Cab is breathtakingly beautiful, especially at this time of year."

I had to agree. Veraison had set in a few days ago, and the vineyards were resplendent with golds, purples, deep reds, lime, and chartreuse green, all against the backdrop of the cadmium of the grape leaves.

There was a tent large enough to hold five hundred people already set up on the main lawn. The old winery wasn't big enough to hold either the ceremony or the reception, but it was where she and I were having dinner tonight after the balloon ride over our vineyards.

Bit, my best man, and Alex, who Daphne had asked to stand up with her, had made all the arrangements, threatening the lives of anyone who dared interrupt our date.

The room we were in looked a lot like it had the night we planned to celebrate our engagement. Lights were strung on the ceiling, our table was illuminated by candles, and around the room, on nearly every surface were bouquets of flowers.

"I'd like to propose a toast," I said after we'd taken our seats and I'd poured us each a glass of wine from the bottle that sat on the table. "To you, the woman this wine is named for."

Her brow furrowed slightly, then we both took a sip. "It's magnificent, Cru."

"I agree. It's the reason I named it Cuvée Daphne."

Her face flushed, and her eyes filled with tears. "I don't deserve you," she murmured like she had so many times in the years I'd known her.

"We belong together, Daph, and that means we deserve each other—which I suppose can be good or bad."

We both chuckled, and I signaled to my brother and sister, letting them know to serve the first of three courses.

After we finished eating and they cleared our dessert plates, the music changed from the soft jazz that played in the background to the song we chose not for our first dance but for our last as an unmarried couple. I stood, pulled out her chair, and held out my hand. "Dance with me?"

You're a sky, a sky full of stars," I sang softly in her ear.

"So, I'm going to give you my heart," she sang back.

"And I'll give you mine," I said since it wasn't part of the lyrics. "Forever, Daphne."

"Forever, Enzo."

Keep reading for a sneak peek at
the next book in Heather Slade's
Wicked Winemakers Central Coast
Second Label series,

Bit's Bliss

**He's a dominant man who's sworn off love.
She's an innocent heiress trapped by betrayal.
Together, they'll build a love
stronger than their scars.**

BIT

I've spent the past year recovering from an attack that nearly killed me, monitoring security feeds, and avoiding human connection. But when Eberly Warwick bids on a date with me at a charity auction, I can't resist the pull of the innocent event planner who's been working at Los Caballeros. Her wide-eyed trust awakens my protective instincts—and darker desires. As her father's disappearance becomes entangled with my violent past, I must risk everything to keep her safe, even as I struggle to resist claiming her completely.

EBERLY

My perfectly planned life implodes when my wedding is called off and my father vanishes, leaving behind a mountain of debt and suspicious business dealings. The only bright spot is Trevino Avila, my silent, watchful boss, who makes me feel safer than I've ever been. But as I uncover layers of deception involving my ex-fiancé and criminal organizations, I must decide if I can trust Bit with not just my safety, but my heart. Between the threat of losing my family home and discovering my father's secrets, I find myself drawn into a world of danger—and the commanding embrace of a man who demands my complete surrender.

1

Bit

315

My sister told me to imagine everyone in the room was naked when I stepped out onto the stage as the last man being auctioned for a date as part of the Wicked Winemakers' Ball's bachelor auction.

There was only one person in the room I could— or wanted—to picture that way. *Eberly.* The woman whose naked body appeared in my dreams and fantasies every day. Hiding my attraction to her was most difficult when we worked side by side at the events we hosted in the original winery building on my family's property.

On her first day in her job as event planner, I'd followed her as she looked around the space inside and out and jotted notes on a pad of paper.

"What did you just write?" I asked when she stuck her pencil behind her ear and smiled.

"We'll call it the Los Caballeros Stonehouse and Gardens."

"We will?" I asked, taking in the sparse and mostly dead grass on every side of the building. "That might be misleading. Are you sure you don't just want to call it the old winery building?"

"Close your eyes," she'd said, and since I'd be willing to do whatever she asked of me, even bark like a dog, I squeezed them shut.

"Imagine the most beautiful gardens you've ever seen in your life."

"Okay."

"Where are they?"

"At the inn in Cambria."

"Right! That's perfect!"

I peeked through one eye, saw her writing something else on the pad, then shut it before she caught me.

"What are your favorite flowers?" she asked.

"I don't know. Roses, I guess."

"Also perfect. In the back, we can make a kitchen garden, and on the side leading into the woods, we could build a wall and call it the secret garden. And here—"

"Eberly, can I open my eyes?"

When she touched my arm, I flinched.

"Sorry," she whispered.

"No, I'm sorry."

She smiled and pointed to the low wall and path that led to the building's entrance. "Can you imagine this space with Eden climbers and ivy covering the stone?"

My eyes scrunched.

"Roses," she said.

"I can't do it," I told her.

"Do what?"

"Imagine."

"Of course you can!"

I shook my head. "Nope."

She'd led me inside that day, and when she told me to picture a couple dancing in the room on their wedding day, I repeated that I couldn't.

"Maybe this will help." She stood in front of me, then put one of my arms around her waist and her hand in my other. "Twirl me around the room," she said.

I stood in place, staring at her.

"Okay, I'll do it."

We went around and around until I felt dizzy, and somewhere along the way, I started spinning her instead of her doing it to me. It was the best day of my life.

When my sister asked me to come up with an idea for a date to auction, it was all I could think of.

"Ladies, you are in for a real treat tonight. For the very first time, you can bid on a date with my brother Trevino!"

I was stunned when people clapped.

"Go ahead," Alex whispered with her hand over the mic. "Do like we practiced."

I stepped forward and stopped at the stage's midpoint.

"Trevino has promised the winning bidder one of the most romantic dates we've ever had at the Wicked Winemakers' Ball. First, a walk on Moonstone Beach, followed by a drive through the hills on the back of his motorcycle—which, by the way, I didn't know he had. When you arrive at Los Caballeros, you'll be swept away on horseback to the Stonehouse and Gardens, where you'll enjoy a private dinner, followed by dancing under the twinkling lights."

I felt my cheeks flush when my eyes met Eberly's. Maybe I went too far.

"Okay, ladies, who wants to start us off with an opening bid of a thousand dollars?"

Eberly raised her paddle. "I'll bid five."

"Five?" asked Alex.

"Thousand."

About the Author

USA Today best-selling author Heather Slade writes shamelessly sexy, edge-of-your seat romantic suspense.

She gave herself the gift of writing a book for her own birthday one year. Sixty-plus books later (and counting), she's having the time of her life.

The women Slade writes are self-confident, strong, with wills of their own, and hearts as big as the Colorado sky. The men are sublimely sexy, seductive alphas who rise to the challenge of capturing the sweet soul of a woman whose heart they'll hold in the palm of their hand forever. Add in a couple of neck-snapping twists and turns, a page-turning mystery, and a swoon-worthy HEA, and you'll be holding one of her books in your hands.

She loves to hear from her readers. You can contact her at heather@heatherslade.com

To keep up with her latest news and releases, please visit her website at www.heatherslade.com to sign up for her newsletter.

MORE FROM AUTHOR HEATHER SLADE

WINE COUNTRY ROMANCE

BUTLER RANCH
Kade's Worth
Brodie's Promise
Maddox's Truce
Naughton's Secret
Mercer's Vow
Kade's Return
Butler Ranch Christmas

WICKED WINEMAKERS
CENTRAL COAST
FIRST LABEL
Brix's Bid
Ridge's Release
Press' Passion
Zin's Sins
Tryst's Temptation

WICKED WINEMAKERS
CENTRAL COAST
SECOND LABEL
Beau's Beloved
Cru's Crush
Bit's Bliss
Snapper's Seduction
Kick's Kiss

WICKED WINEMAKERS
RUSSIAN RIVER VALLEY
FIRST LABEL
Bas' Blend
Hux's Harvest
Wolf's Want
Oak's Vintage
Cooper's Claim

COWBOY ROMANCE

COWBOYS OF
CRESTED BUTTE
A Cowboy Falls
A Cowboy's Dance
A Cowboy's Kiss
A Cowboy Stays
A Cowboy Wins

ROARING FORK RANCH
Roaring Fork Wrangler
Roaring Fork Roughstock
Roaring Fork Rockstar
Roaring Fork Rooker
Roaring Fork Bridger

SANGRE VISTA RANCH
Thorn's Stand
Stetson's Storm
Maverick's Reckoning
Cinch's Wager
Flints Chance